Samuel French Acting Edition

Kingdom Come

by Jenny Rachel Weiner

I0591846

ıl SAMUEL FRENCH lı

SAMUELFRENCH.COM   SAMUELFRENCH.CO.UK

FOR PRODUCTION ENQUIRIES

UNITED STATES AND CANADA
Info@SamuelFrench.com
1-866-598-8449

UNITED KINGDOM AND EUROPE
Plays@SamuelFrench.co.uk
020-7255-4302

Each title is subject to availability from Samuel French, depending upon country of performance. Please be aware that *KINGDOM COME* may not be licensed by Samuel French in your territory. Professional and amateur producers should contact the nearest Samuel French office or licensing partner to verify availability.

MUSIC USE NOTE

IMPORTANT BILLING AND CREDIT REQUIREMENTS

KINGDOM COME had its world premiere produced in New York City by Roundabout Theatre Company (Todd Haimes, Artistic Director; Harold Wolpert, Managing Director; Julia C. Levy, Executive Director; Sydney Beers, General Manager) as part of Roundabout Underground at the Harold and Miriam Steinberg Center for Theatre on November 3, 2016. The cast was as follows:

SAMANTHA CARLIN. . . . . Carmen M. Herlihy

DELORES AQUENDO. . . . . Socorro Santiago

LAYNE FALCONE . . . . .Crystal Finn

SUZ MILLER . . . . Stephanie Styles

DOMINICK AQUENDO. . . . . Alex Hernandez

CHARACTERS

SAMANTHA CARLIN – (F, thirties) Samantha has mousy hair so thin you can see her scalp. The bed Samantha lives in is raised and has large guardrails that protect her from falling out. Samantha weighs approximately 600 pounds and is mostly confined to her bed. It takes most of the effort she has to move from one room to another, so she usually doesn't – she shits into a pan, pees into a catheter, is scrubbed down to get clean, and eats when food is brought to her. She has been this way since she was eighteen. Before that, Samantha wheeled herself around in a wheelchair. Before that she walked, but her knees hurt. Also plays **KINGDOMCOME42**.

DELORES AQUENDO – (F, forty-nine) Samantha's health aide. She was hired by Samantha's mom. She's been working for Samantha for about a year. Originally from Colombia. She is obsessed with her son.

LAYNE FALCONE – (F, thirty-three) Layne [Lay-*nee*] is lonely and suffers from anxiety. Layne is an office assistant at an insurance company. She wears nude stockings every day and neutral skirt-suits from Ross Dress For Less. Layne is the kind of girl nobody sees. Layne lives alone. She cooks alone. She sleeps alone. She prays alone. She sings alone. She thinks alone. Also plays **DELAYEDFLIGHT82**.

SUZ MILLER – (F, twenty-three) Layne's coworker at Hensher Insurance Agency. Suz is a ditz and a party girl, but somewhere underneath all the rhinestones and eye shadow is a good heart. She's bubbly like champagne, but like the really shitty kind from the corner deli. Also plays **SYDLOVES4545** and **WANNAPLAYWIDME88**.

DOMINICK AQUENDO – (M, thirties) A hot, simple, seemingly vapid Latino man. He is Delores' son. He knows how to use his looks to get what he wants. He's an "actor/model" in LA, but is actually a busboy at a bakery. Also plays **SOCCERCOACH983**, **SPRINGSTEINLOVENJ**, and **YOGADAD123**.

SETTING

A city thirty miles south of Las Vegas: Carson City, Nevada.
Later, Los Angeles

TIME

Present Day

AUTHOR'S NOTES

The Internet in this play begins as a literal projection of what the characters see on their screen, but becomes highly theatrical once Layne and Samantha meet. It's important that the actors don't pretend to type or see computer screens once they enter into their world; they are transported when they shift to their alternate personas – they speak how one would speak aloud, not exact pronunciations of the lingo they type, but we should see their online conversations projected in some way. The "real world" is naturalistic and the online world hyper-naturalistic – a kind of poetry jutting up against the mundane.

PROJECTIONS NOTE:

Everything that happens on the Internet is intended to be projected, and the chats should all be spoken aloud, unless indicated. As the women become more entrenched in their fantasy world, you can feel free to play with how realistic the projections are and how much of the actual text we see.

SPECIAL THANKS:

I'd like to thank Cusi Cram, Matthew Maguire, Mark Bly, and Elliot Fox at Fordham University/Primary Stages who gave me the confidence and room to write this play. To my generous friends and colleagues who read drafts and gave feedback along the way. To Todd Haimes, Julia Levy, Robyn Goodman, Josh Fiedler, and my hero Jill Rafson for giving me a forever theatre home. To my inimitable director and friend Kip Fagan: you seriously rock. And to my family, who gives me the courage, strength, and chutzpah to follow my dreams.

Scene One

(Lights up on **SAMANTHA** *and* **DELORES** *watching a game show.)*

*(***SAMANTHA*** *is in bed, and* **DELORES** *is propped up against its side.* **SAMANTHA***'s bed is raised and has large guardrails that protect her from falling out.* **SAMANTHA** *weighs approximately 600 pounds and is mostly confined to this spot.)*

(The screen illuminates **SAMANTHA***'s face.)*

(We hear an opening theme song.*)

ANNOUNCER. Theresa Dioluca!

SAMANTHA & DELORES. Come on down!

ANNOUNCER. Heather Catarucci!

SAMANTHA & DELORES. Come on down!

ANNOUNCER. Frank Cohen-Weinberg!

SAMANTHA & DELORES. Come on down!

ANNOUNCER. And here's your host!

...

ANNOUNCER, SAMANTHA & DELORES. DREW CAREY!

*(***SAMANTHA*** *and* **DELORES** *watch the show.)*

DELORES. You know…

The Price Is Right shoots in LA.

Maybe someday we can go together.

That's where my Dominick lives.

SAMANTHA. *(Lighthearted.)* Yeah, you told me.

---

*A license to produce *Kingdom Come* does not include a performance license for the use of any specific game show theme song. The publisher and author suggest that the licensee create an original composition. For further information, please see Music Use Note on page 3.

I don't have Alzheimer's I'm just fat, Delores.

DELORES. How should I know if you hear me when I talk?

SAMANTHA. *(In* The Price Is Right *announcer voice.)* Ladies and Gentlemen, here we have Delores Aquendo from Bogota, Colombia!

Give her a round of applause!

> **(DELORES** *cheers.)*

She's forty-nine, though she looks thirty-five.

DELORES. Bless you.

SAMANTHA. She enjoys Salsa music and complaining about the temperature!

DELORES. I'm going through changes! It's not my fault!

SAMANTHA. She has a son named Dom.

Who's an actor in LA.

And also is a busboy.

DELORES. Employee of the Month THIS MONTH!

SAMANTHA. She loves Ruby Tuesday's never-ending salad bar.

Let's hear it one more time for Delores!

> *(They both cheer.)*

DELORES. What would I do without you?

> **(SAMANTHA** *smiles.)*

SAMANTHA. Hey didja get my scratchies?

DELORES. Oh, yes!

> **(DELORES** *pulls out a handful of scratch-off lottery tickets. She pulls out two quarters. They scratch.)*

Ugh. I'm bad luck I think.

> *(She spits three times over her shoulder.)*

Anything?

SAMANTHA. Five bucks!

> *(She shows* **DELORES** *the winning card.)*

DELORES. Look at you! Twice in one week!

SAMANTHA. I'm rich!

DELORES. I can't wait to tell your mama how lucky you've been. Maybe I'll get a raise.

SAMANTHA. Don't involve her.

DELORES. Why? She'll be so happy!

SAMANTHA. How could you tell with all the botox?

DELORES. Enough, you.

SAMANTHA. What? It always looks like she has to take a shit.

>   *(She pulls her face back so she looks like she has botox.)*

"Be right back!"

DELORES. *(Laughing.)* Stop it!

>   *(More serious.)*

Your face will stick that way!

>   *(**SAMANTHA** laughs and then starts to cough.)*

>   *(**DELORES** brings a glass of water and a straw to her lips.)*

SAMANTHA. *(Hoarse.)* I hate her.

>   *(**DELORES** touches **SAMANTHA**'s hair.)*

DELORES. Lemme do something with this.

SAMANTHA. Why?

DELORES. You'll look so pretty. Just like Jennifer Lopez!

SAMANTHA. I don't think that's a realistic goal.

DELORES. Why don't we do a makeover! Wouldn't that be fun?

SAMANTHA. Fun for who?

DELORES. Come on. Let's make you up!

SAMANTHA. You're gonna have to work pretty hard.

DELORES. Tsk. Shh. What do I always say about you have to love yourself.

What do I *always say*.

I listen to Deepak Chopra. I know.

SAMANTHA. Fine.

DELORES. Yay!

SAMANTHA. *(Rhetorical.)* What else am I doing?

DELORES. Let me do some Reiki on you first.

SAMANTHA. Aw, man.

DELORES. You'll feel muy bien.

SAMANTHA. *Judge Judy*'s up next.

DELORES. She won't mind.

> (**DELORES** *begins to practice Reiki on* **SAMANTHA** *as the lights come down.*)

Scene Two

(**LAYNE** *sits on the floor underneath her desk.*)

(*It's after hours at work; most of the lights are off, except for a few fluorescents.*)

(**SUZ** *appears – she's wearing "going out" clothes: A mini-skirt, a belly shirt, and four-inch stilettos.*)

(*She has lipstick smeared on her face.*)

(*She might be a little drunk.*)

(*She is curling her eyelashes as she enters.*)

(**LAYNE** *has headphones in; she's listening to a guided meditation.*)

LAYNE. I choose to release the fears I have projected onto my body.

I am willing to see my body with love.

I release my ego's fear now.

I choose to see my body as love.

I choose to release my fears.

I am ready to see love.

I am innocent.

I am love.

SUZ. You know those things they barely work.

LAYNE. *(Caught off guard.)* Oh sorry? I didn't –

SUZ. I tried once I did a whole month of that crap with the meditation and the raw vegan cheez and those patches? You know the patches you put on your uterus?

LAYNE. No.

SUZ. Really?

(*Beat.*)

Anyway, for a whole month I was Buddhist – doctor's orders – and at the end I was just hungry and needed a shower.

LAYNE. Oh um I don't know.

SUZ. The things we stress about *we* create. Money? Self-afflicting. Government? For the birds! My dad was in the army and we traveled everywhere and I got to *see*, you know, I got to see the country. And it's not pretty. So don't look, Layne.

LAYNE. Okay.

SUZ. Mr. Hensher doesn't like when we listen to music at our desks by the way.

So.

Don't do it.

Consider this your warning.

LAYNE. But it's after hours.

SUZ. I'm just GIVING YOU A TIP.

It's like really, really nice of me.

> (*SUZ takes a picture of herself with a duck face right in the middle of their conversation.*)

LAYNE. What are you doing?

SUZ. Snapchatting what does it look like?

LAYNE. Is that a game?

SUZ. Oh God. You really are like a sad old lady.

LAYNE. I'm thirty-three.

SUZ. Like a little sad old bird with a broken leg. And like an eye that's moving in a million directions. You're a sad bird who can't fly. Poor thing.

What are you still doing here anyway? It's like 10:00 at night. Ohmygod are you homeless. Do you *live* at Hensher? That's why you always wear the same grey suit everyday! I knew it!

LAYNE. I'm not homeless, Suz! I just missed the last JAC. I'll take a cab or something.

SUZ. "Jump Around Carson" is the lamest name I've *ever* heard for an *official bus system*. GOD GET ME OUT OF THIS HELL HOLE!

LAYNE. Do you want to try my meditations?

SUZ. NO!

("Jump Around" by House of Pain starts playing on **SUZ**'s phone as she begins jumping around spastically. Her dancing is bad but also a little sexy. She sings. After a few lines:)*

LAYNE. I know this one!

SUZ. *(To **LAYNE**.)* COME ON!

*(**LAYNE** starts singing and dancing too. Her dancing is terrible.)*

SUZ. *(Laughing.)* You *do* look like a weird old bird!

*(**SUZ** starts filming **LAYNE**. **LAYNE** really plays up the bird dancing.)*

This is so funny. Everyone's gonna love it.

LAYNE. Everyone? Who are you showing it to?

SUZ. I sent it to the whole office.

LAYNE. Suz!

*(**SUZ** turns off the music.)*

SUZ. Don't worry. This will give you some real street cred around here. Believe me.

LAYNE. Okay.

SUZ. That was cool. You're not as lame as I thought.

*(**LAYNE** squawks.)*

Nevermind.

Who takes the bus in Carson City anyway?

LAYNE. I don't drive.

I used to, but.

---

*A license to produce *Kingdom Come* does not include a performance license for "Jump Around." The publisher and author suggest that the licensee contact ASCAP or BMI to ascertain the music publisher and contact such music publisher to license or acquire permission for performance of the song. If a license or permission is unattainable for "Jump Around," the licensee may not use the song in *Kingdom Come*, but may create an original composition in a similar style or use a similar song in the public domain. For further information, please see Music Use Note on page 3.

Then I watched this *very graphic* documentary about airbags and now I can't be in a car without seeing my disfigured, mangled body.

Um.

Are you gonna write me up for being here late or whatever?

SUZ. Me? No no no no no. I am just *supposed* to tell if I see anything.

Me and Rob are like kinda close, so.

LAYNE. Cool.

SUZ. He's fifty-six.

LAYNE. Huh.

SUZ. I'm twenty-three.

LAYNE. Oh, *I* don't care.

SUZ. Do you care about *anything?*

LAYNE. Sure.

SUZ. What?!

LAYNE. *(She seems genuinely scared.)* I don't know?

SUZ. I'm sorry, I'm being a bitch.

Something really intense just happened.

> *(She waits for* **LAYNE** *to ask what it is. She doesn't.)*
>
> *(***SUZ*** cozies up to* **LAYNE**.*)*

I just had the worst fight with Rob in his office.

I was hysterical.

LAYNE. Oh. I'm sorry –

SUZ. Do you have a boyfriend?

LAYNE. Nope.

SUZ. Why?

LAYNE. Oh uh I don't know.

SUZ. When was your last relationship?

LAYNE. Um. I can't remember.

SUZ. I'm *sure* I have someone I could set you up with. Hmm.

Lemme think lemme think lemme think.

(She takes a long time, really thinking about it.)

I don't, I'm sorry.

LAYNE. It's okay.

SUZ. Everyone I know is online. I mean it's the only way to date now. Three of my friends just got married and they all met their husbands on Tinder, happn, and Bumble.

LAYNE. Oh.

SUZ. Wanna go to the bar down the street and get blackout with me?

LAYNE. I don't think so.

SUZ. Why not? It'll be fun.

(She goes to reach.) I think I have an extra tube top in my bag.

LAYNE. No, that's okay!

SUZ. Don't you want to bond?

We see each other every day and I barely know anything about you.

LAYNE. There's not much to know.

SUZ. I really feel like we could be friends.

I've always sort of had that instinct.

And an actual psychic once told me that *I'm* sort of psychic, so. Trust me.

Come ouuuuuutttttt.

LAYNE. That's really sweet, Suz. But I'm just not a going out person.

SUZ. It seems like you're very sad.

LAYNE. I'm not.

SUZ. You look like you're about to cry.

I literally *can't* cry. I have dry eye syndrome.

(Beat.)

Life moves pretty fast, Layne. If you don't turn around and look sometimes, you're definitely not gonna see it.

LAYNE. Are you quoting Ferris Bueller?

SUZ. No.

LAYNE. Okay.

Goodnight, Suz.

SUZ. Goodnight Elaine.

LAYNE. That's not my name.

Scene Three

(SAMANTHA sits up in bed.)

(She browses the Internet.)

(She logs onto her OkCupid profile, which has a picture of a beautiful Latino man.)

(She adds to the profile:)

SAMANTHA: "yo ladies! Dom here. was just awarded Employee of the Month at my bakery. dreams do come true ;)"

(DELORES walks in with SAMANTHA's dinner, chipper.)

(SAMANTHA quickly shuts her computer.)

DELORES. Sammy! Dinner!

SAMANTHA. Ooh, yay!

DELORES. Are you watching the YouTube?

I have to show you a video of this funny boy from *Ellen.* Dom sent it to me.

He met Ellen once, did I ever tell you that?

SAMANTHA. You did.

DELORES. She told him he was handsome.

Can you believe it? My own son!

He was there seeing Three Eyes Blind. That's his favorite band.

Let's put on the video.

It'll make you laugh I know it.

SAMANTHA. I'm starving can I have my food now?

(DELORES hesitantly hands SAMANTHA her food.)

(It's something healthy, like grilled chicken and broccoli.)

I DON'T WANT THIS SHIT, Delores! Fuck!

DELORES. Oh, come on Sammy, please.
Just try it.

SAMANTHA. I asked for a Coney Island dog, a large fry, and a Coke. You know I need it or I get a headache!

DELORES. I'm trying to help you!

SAMANTHA. I don't need your help!

DELORES. *(Under her breath.)* Eso es pura mierda.

SAMANTHA. I TOLD YOU NOT TO DO THAT.

DELORES. Shh, shh. It's okay. I'm sorry.

> *(**DELORES** goes into the kitchen and grabs a greasy fast food bag.)*
>
> *(She hands it to **SAMANTHA**.)*

SAMANTHA. Thank you.

> *(**SAMANTHA** devours her food.)*
>
> *(Beat.)*

DELORES. *(About the YouTube video.)* It's still loading.

SAMANTHA. *(With her mouth full.)* Fine.

DELORES. Scootch –

> *(**DELORES** sits on the guardrail and props **SAMANTHA**'s computer onto **SAMANTHA**'s belly. She finds the YouTube video. **SAMANTHA** eats her dinner while **DELORES** sips out of a plastic cup with a scrunchy straw. Lights dim on **SAMANTHA** and **DELORES**.)*
>
> *(Lights up on **LAYNE** in her apartment. She's making an online dating profile for LayneF82.)*
>
> *(She types:)*

LAYNE: Hey, I'm Layne.
I'm thirty-three years old and I like to cook.
My biggest fear is being forced to jump out of a window.

> *(**LAYNE** deletes that sentence.)*

(She fixes her hair.)

(Wipes underneath her eyes.)

(Then she brings up the camera on her computer.)

(She takes a selfie – duck lips and seductive eyes, reminiscent of the photo **SUZ** *took earlier.)*

(Flash!)

(It's horrible.)

WHAT ARE YOU DOING LAYNE?!

*(***LAYNE*** *types into the search bar:)*

(Hot But Sweet Girl.)

(Thousands of pictures come up.)

*(***LAYNE*** *scrolls through the photos. She comes upon a girl who she finds suitable. She drags the picture into the photo section of her new profile, replacing the picture of her real face.)*

(She changes the occupation on her profile to Stewardess and the name of her profile to DelayedFlight82.)

(She types:)

DELAYEDFLIGHT82: Hey, I'm Courtney.

My favorite thing to do is bungee jump. I've been six times. I'm obsessed.

My dream is to go to every country in the world. And learn how to speak at least six languages before I die. I'm getting close.

I want to know what it feels like to sing in front of millions of people.

I want to shave my head and not care what anybody thinks and wear long dangly earrings that brush up against my shoulders when I dance.

I'm kind. I listen.

I have a freckle next to my belly button that looks like a heart.

I can't listen to Judy Garland without weeping. My dad and I used to sing "For Me and My Gal" every night before bed.

The six things I couldn't live without: family, friends, love, music, movies, peanut butter.

The thing I'm most embarrassed to admit is that I'm on this site.

[Lights dim on **LAYNE**.*]*

[Lights back up on **SAMANTHA**, *alone.]*

[She gets an alert.]

[Two New Messages!]

[She opens them up.]

SYDLOVES4545:

From **SYDLOVES4545**

Sent at 7:04 a.m.

Hey Dom! I'm Sydney. You might not guess from looking at my pictures, but I also still sleep with a stuffed animal! His name is Rhino and he has been sown up probably about fifty times. I think it's really sweet that you still have Mr. Ted. Most guys who look like you definitely wouldn't admit that lol. Let me know if you wanna go out sometime. You prolly won't respond since most guys on here don't lol. But if you want more pics I can send them. – Sydney

*[*SAMANTHA *responds:]*

KINGDOMCOME42:

From **kingDOMcome42**

Sent at 8:24 p.m.

Hey Sydney! thank u so much for your message! u seem amazing n I would be lucky 2 have someone like u in my life. It's rude not 2 respond and women like you don't deserve it. i'm sorry on behalf of all men. Ur putting urself out there n that's amazing. Nvr change. I'm actually going to be out of the

country doing **AIDS** work in Africa for the next six months, so we probably can't ever meet. Give Rhino a squeeze 4 me! Off to the gym! Peace n' Love – Dom

WANNAPLAYWIDME88:

From **WANNAPLAYWIDME88**

Sent at 1:33 p.m.

Hey big boi ur hawt I think we could get dirty and play lemme know if u wanna try i have lots of ideas 4 us lol

KINGDOMCOME42:

From **kingDOMcome42**

Sent at 8:26 p.m.

thnx but I don't go for girls like you. I think u should give yourself more respect and think of yourself higher than you do. u don't need to degrade urself to have men respect you or think ur beautiful. Just be u. It's enough. God bless u. Off to the gym. Peace! – Dom

[We move back to **LAYNE***.]*

[She sends a message to SoccerCoach983.]

DELAYEDFLIGHT82: heya coach!

[SoccerCoach983 signs off.]

LAYNE. Must have clicked something.

[She sends a message to SpringsteenloveNJ.]

DELAYEDFLIGHT82: Hello there. Have you ever seen Bruce live? He's AWESOME!

SPRINGSTEENLOVENJ: yeah i have 203 times actually u?

DELAYEDFLIGHT82: Just once in the 80's.

[SpringsteenloveNJ signs off.]

DELAYEDFLIGHT82: hello?

[She sends a message to yogadad123.]

DELAYEDFLIGHT82: Om!

YOGADAD123: I wanna spin you around like spaghetti on a fork and then stuff you in my mouth.

> *[**LAYNE** hits the Block button.]*
>
> *[She shudders.]*
>
> *[She sees kingDOMcome42's profile.]*
>
> *[**SAMANTHA** gets a notification.]*
>
> *["DelayedFlight82 wants to chat."]*
>
> *[She accepts.]*
>
> *[Lights up on both **SAMANTHA** and **LAYNE** for the first time.]*
>
> *[We enter into a different kind of space now – the world of the Internet – pure fantasy and projection. The women speak their chat aloud while the words, a specific speak only suitable for the screen, are also projected for the audience to see.]*

DELAYEDFLIGHT82: Hey!

KINGDOMCOME42: hey you.

DELAYEDFLIGHT82: How are you?

KINGDOMCOME42: doin pretty well cutie, u?

DELAYEDFLIGHT82: I'm at the airport, bored. Trying to figure out what to eat.

KINGDOMCOME42: well what r u in the mood for?

DELAYEDFLIGHT77: Maybe Chinese? Or Mexican?

KINGDOMCOME42: both fine choices

DELAYEDFLIGHT82: Thank you!!!!

> *[**LAYNE** winces at her response.]*

KINGDOMCOME42: what r u doing there?

DELAYEDFLIGHT82: I have a layover. I'm a stewardess.

KINGDOMCOME42: rnt u supposed 2 say flight attendant nowadays?

DELAYEDFLIGHT82: Oh, yeah! You're right. PC!

KINGDOMCOME42: lol. got other pix?

DELAYEDFLIGHT82: I don't know how to work this thing! Let me take a look.

DELAYEDFLIGHT82: Check now? I think I fixed it.

KINGDOMCOME42: oh i see them. cool. brb.

[SAMANTHA browses LAYNE's pictures.]

[They all look vaguely like the same person.]

KINGDOMCOME42: your name's Courtney?

DELAYEDFLIGHT82: Yep. And you're Dom?

KINGDOMCOME42: short for dominick, after my Grandpa.

DELAYEDFLIGHT82: That's a great name. You're really cute.

KINGDOMCOME42: aw thanks. That's really nice. u seem pretty cool yourself.

DELAYEDFLIGHT82: Really?

KINGDOMCOME42: ur beautiful. any guy wud b lucky 2 have u

DELAYEDFLIGHT82: Thank you.

KINGDOMCOME42: my pleasure. so ur a flight attendant. always on the move I guess?

DELAYEDFLIGHT82: It's a really cool job, actually. I get to meet a lot of people

DELAYEDFLIGHT82: I get to travel the world which is awesome and my passion.

KINGDOMCOME42: have u always wanted to travel?

DELAYEDFLIGHT82: Ever since I was a little girl. I followed my dream.

KINGDOMCOME42: that's really inspiring.

DELAYEDFLIGHT82: thanks. So you're a pastry chef?

KINGDOMCOME42: yeah

DELAYEDFLIGHT82: COOL

[All-caps was accidental.]

DELAYEDFLIGHT82: where do you live?

KINGDOMCOME42: L.A.

DELAYEDFLIGHT82: oh that's weird, aren't we matched by location?

KINGDOMCOME42: we must just be a rly good match ;)

DELAYEDFLIGHT82: "Meant to be" HAHA

KINGDOMCOME42: where do u live?

DELAYEDFLIGHT82: Carson City, Nevada

KINGDOMCOME42: my mom lives in carson!

DELAYEDFLIGHT82: crazy!!!!

DELAYEDFLIGHT82: r u at work?

KINGDOMCOME42: I just got home.

DELAYEDFLIGHT82: me 2.

KINGDOMCOME42: u live at the airport?

DELAYEDFLIGHT82: Oh, I mean sort of it feels like home I guess.

KINGDOMCOME42: totally. that's how I feel about my bakery.

DELAYEDFLIGHT82: Sweets are my total weakness.

DELAYEDFLIGHT82: I would be a million pounds if I were a pastry chef.

KINGDOMCOME42: o yeah tell me about it. i hit the gym every day to avoid that lol.

DELAYEDFLIGHT82: I wanna try your cupcakes! Red velvet are my absolute favorite.

KINGDOMCOME42: mine too!

KINGDOMCOME42: my mom used 2 get me this cake w/ red velvet and funfetti sprinkles

KINGDOMCOME42: she would serve it at my birthday party every yr

DELAYEDFLIGHT82: I never had any birthday parties.

KINGDOMCOME42: how come?

DELAYEDFLIGHT82: Dad worked a lot. We didn't have a lot of $$.

KINGDOMCOME42: what about ur mom?

DELAYEDFLIGHT82: She died when we were little

KINGDOMCOME42: o i'm sorry

DELAYEDFLIGHT82: It's ok – do you have a girlfriend?

KINGDOMCOME42: nope.

DELAYEDFLIGHT82: that's crazy. how come?

KINGDOMCOME42: dunno. most girls I meet r phony.

DELAYEDFLIGHT82: me too lol

KINGDOMCOME42: you probably meet all kinds of people.

KINGDOMCOME42: y don't u have n e one? your gorgeous.

DELAYEDFLIGHT82: Thanks I'm shy I guess.

DELAYEDFLIGHT82: What does your screenname mean?

KINGDOMCOME42: well my name is dom so that's part of it

DELAYEDFLIGHT82: totally

KINGDOMCOME42: and i just rly love that verse in the bible u kno

KINGDOMCOME42: whats waiting 4 us

KINGDOMCOME42: the next world

KINGDOMCOME42: its something 2 look 4wrd 2 i guess

DELAYEDFLIGHT82: that's beautiful

KINGDOMCOME42: thnx

KINGDOMCOME42: i'm glad u messaged me

DELAYEDFLIGHT82: me too.

KINGDOMCOME42: where did u travel today, DelayedFlight?

DELAYEDFLIGHT82: lol. Fiji

KINGDOMCOME42: that's amazing. i've always wanted 2 go there, actually.

KINGDOMCOME42: i hear the beaches are incredible.

DELAYEDFLIGHT82: they are. the sand is so soft, you want to wear it like a coat.

DELAYEDFLIGHT82: maybe you can come with me someday.

> *[*SAMANTHA *smiles.]*

> *[So does* LAYNE.*]*

KINGDOMCOME42: i'd like that.

Scene Four

> (**LAYNE** *is in the office breakroom with* **SUZ.**)
>
> (**LAYNE** *feverishly types on her phone.*)
>
> (*She laughs and blushes.*)

SUZ. And then she just walked out! I was like, Kiki, we're all trying to lose this holiday weight, okay? None of us *want to be going to Killer Abs*, none of us want to be on this *two week juice cleanse*. I don't know how Gwyneth does it. She's really learned to balance it all, you know. GOOP is like my *bible* right now. SUCH an inspiration.

> (*Beat.*)

Hello?

LAYNE. Huh?

SUZ. Isn't that so rude.

LAYNE. Totally.

SUZ. (*Indicating the phone.*) Who's that?

LAYNE. What?

SUZ. Who are you talking to?

LAYNE. Nobody.

SUZ. I've never seen you text.

LAYNE. You only started paying attention to me like two weeks ago.

SUZ. So?

Who do you text?

You don't text me.

LAYNE. People. I text people.

SUZ. So who is this person?

LAYNE. It's no big deal, he's just some guy.

SUZ. SOME GUY?! LAYNE!

> (**SUZ** *hugs* **LAYNE.**)
>
> (*She aggressively jumps her around.*)

Ahh! This is so exciting!

I can't wait to tell everyone!

We have bets in the office on whether you'll be alone forever!

LAYNE. I don't want to make a big deal about it yet.

    (Brushing it off.)

It's just like some dumb thing, you know?

SUZ. So...where did you meet him?

LAYNE. I don't wanna say.

SUZ. TELL ME!

LAYNE. I met him online, okay?

SUZ. YOU LISTENED TO MY ADVICE!

    (A realization.)

I should be a life coach.

LAYNE. I'm just trying it out. We'll see how it goes.

SUZ. See? Online dating totally works! I used to think it was only for freaks who killed animals for fun when they were kids, but that's not true anymore!

LAYNE. Yeah, I mean, it's still kinda new, but we just totally connect.

SUZ. What's his name?

LAYNE. *(She giddy smiles.)* Dom.

SUZ. Layne. You are *so* in love.

You have to do whatever it takes to make this work.

LAYNE. He's amazing.

We talk every night. All night.

I haven't gotten any sleep at all, but I've never felt *so awake.*

I'm a cliché! I don't care!

I mean he's just so...in tune, you know?

He's sensitive, he loves his mom, he asks questions!

Can you believe that?

And he has the coolest job. He's a pastry chef at a bakery called Le Madeleine.

Isn't that so romantic? *Le Madeleine.*

We actually talked about going to France together someday.

SUZ. Where does this alien come from? AND DOES HE
     HAVE A BROTHER??

LAYNE. He was born in Colombia.

     But he lives in LA now.

SUZ. *(She clicks her teeth.)* Oh, shit.

LAYNE. What?

SUZ. Long distance. You need to shut it down.

LAYNE. Wow, Suz. Really changed your tune there.

SUZ. It's not worth it, believe me. You don't even know him.

LAYNE. I do know him. We have amazing conversations.

SUZ. Like?

LAYNE. Okay, like today we were talking about...well that's
     a stupid –

     And then he told me about this thing he was...

          (SUZ looks at LAYNE like she has two heads.)

     It doesn't make sense out of context.

          (LAYNE goes back to her phone.)

          (She types.)

          (She smiles when she sees the response.)

          (She types again.)

          (She laughs out loud.)

     Oh my God.

SUZ. What?

LAYNE. He just sent me a new picture.

SUZ. Lemme see.

LAYNE. No!

SUZ. Why??

LAYNE. Because it's private.

SUZ. Nothing is private anymore, ever heard of the *Cloud?*
     Show me!

LAYNE. Fine. But don't freak out or anything.

SUZ. Okay.

          (LAYNE shows SUZ a picture of DOM.)

(It's one of those selfies in the mirror. A chair is covering his genitals. His face is kinda blurry. It really could be anyone.)

AHH! OH MY GOD!

(LAYNE runs around the room screaming.)

HE'S SO HOT! WHAT THE FUCK!

LAYNE. I know!

SUZ. I can't believe you're sending sexy pics already!

LAYNE. It's just what's happening naturally.

SUZ. Are you guys gonna meet in person?

LAYNE. We're saving that.

SUZ. But you've video chatted.

LAYNE. The camera is broken on his laptop.

SUZ. Oh Jesus.

LAYNE. What?

SUZ. *(As in "no.")* Uh-uh.

LAYNE. He's busy at the bakery, he hasn't had time to get it fixed.

SUZ. He's a middle school boy in Texas.

LAYNE. Why would you say something like that.

SUZ. Because I'm probably right.

LAYNE. This is real.

I don't know how else to explain it.

SUZ. Just try not to get murdered, okay?

You're my favorite work friend.

LAYNE. I'll do my best.

(LAYNE's phone buzzes. She looks at it.)

Oh! Dom says hi.

SUZ. Hi, Dom!

(To LAYNE, flattered.)

You told him about me.

LAYNE. He sent us a video to watch.

He always sends me the funniest videos.

(**LAYNE** *pulls up the video of the boy from* Ellen*
that **DELORES** *and* **SAMANTHA** *watched earlier.*)

(**LAYNE** *and* **SUZ** *laugh together as they watch the
video.*)

(**SUZ** *looks at* **LAYNE.** **LAYNE** *smiles big.*)

---

*In the original production of *Kingdom Come,* the creators created audio
themselves, similar to audio that might be from *The Ellen Degeneres Show.*
The publisher and author suggest that licensees do the same.

Scene Five

(Early morning.)

(SAMANTHA sits in her bed watching TV and eating a pack of blue sour straws.)

(A game show is playing.)

(We see the light of the TV reflected onto SAMANTHA's face.)

(SAMANTHA accidentally knocks the remote off the bed.)

(She hoists herself up from the bars atop the bed and attempts to get off to retrieve the remote.)

(It takes a painfully long time.)

(Once she's standing, SAMANTHA moves to get the clicker, but she can't reach it.)

(She kneels down, but cries out in pain.)

(DELORES enters through the front door, keys in hand, jacket on, purse slung over her shoulder.)

DELORES. Sammy, what are you doing?!
Let me help you.

SAMANTHA. I'm fine! I wanna do it by myself.

(SAMANTHA gets the remote.)

(She climbs back into bed.)

DELORES. Hi baby.

SAMANTHA. Hi.

DELORES. You sleep okay?

SAMANTHA. Yeah.

DELORES. Any dreams?

SAMANTHA. Can't remember.

DELORES. When you do, you tell me.
You know I'm a dream specialist?

SAMANTHA. Are not.

DELORES. Back home in my country the whole town would come to me to get their palms read.

SAMANTHA. You read palms too?

DELORES. Of course.

SAMANTHA. Are you also a witch?

DELORES. Dios no lo quiera!

(*She crosses herself.*)

What are you eating?

SAMANTHA. Nothing.

DELORES. Your mouth is blue, what were you eating?

SAMANTHA. I wasn't eating anything.

DELORES. (*She points to* **SAMANTHA**'s *mouth.*) AZUL!

(**SAMANTHA** *shows* **DELORES** *the sour straws.*)

Where did you get those?

SAMANTHA. I have a stash. It's how I make sure I don't die while you're gone.

DELORES. Yeesh Sammy.

Don't say things like that.

SAMANTHA. Are you going somewhere after work? You look nice.

DELORES. Why thank you.

I'm celebrating, wanna know why?

SAMANTHA. Sure.

DELORES. My Dommy is here!

SAMANTHA. (*Fearful.*) What?

DELORES. Dom is in Carson City!

SAMANTHA. Dom is *here?*

DELORES. You need to clean your ears? He has a little time off before his next shoot so he's visiting his mama. Isn't that wonderful? I'm taking him to that new Italian restaurant down the street! It's called B'Sghettis!

SAMANTHA. I can't believe it.

DELORES. What's wrong?

SAMANTHA. I just think it's weird, that's all.

He's been saying he's gonna visit for years and he just like never shows up so I didn't expect him to actually like ever grace us with his presence.

DELORES. Are you jealous, mi angél?

SAMANTHA. NO, Delores!

DELORES. Are you nervous to meet him? Because he's a famous actor?

SAMANTHA. He's a busboy at a bakery.

DELORES. THAT'S HIS DAY JOB!

SAMANTHA. He's done two infomercials and a spot for used cars.

DELORES. And a TON of print ads.

SAMANTHA. Okay.

DELORES. He's in Carson through the week.

And he's gonna help out for a few days.

SAMANTHA. Here?

DELORES. He needs some extra money this month. Is that okay with you?

SAMANTHA. I don't know what he'll do. We have a pretty steady routine, Delores.

DELORES. We'll think of something, I'm sure.

SAMANTHA. Fine.

DELORES. Don't be mad, Sammy.

I'm so happy to have my baby here. I'm so happy for him to meet you.

SAMANTHA. Better not leave him here for too long.

He might fall in love with me.

DELORES. Don't I know it!

(**SAMANTHA** *coughs.*)

(*She presses down on her liver.*)

SAMANTHA. Ow.

DELORES. What happened?

SAMANTHA. Just a weird jabbing.

Who knows.

DELORES. In the same place from last time?

      (**SAMANTHA** *nods.*)

  I'll give the doctor a call, okay?

  You want me to call your mama?

SAMANTHA. No.

DELORES. Let's give you something for the pain.

SAMANTHA. Thanks.

      (**DELORES** *gives her something.*)

DELORES. Why don't we get you cozy.

  You can take a rest.

      (**DELORES** *lowers* **SAMANTHA**'s *bed down so she's lying more horizontal.*)

SAMANTHA. Thank you, Delores.

DELORES. No problem, Sweetie.

      (*She puts her lips to* **SAMANTHA**'s *forehead.*)

  No fever.

      (**DELORES** *strokes* **SAMANTHA**'s *forehead.*)

SAMANTHA. That feels nice.

DELORES. Just rest honey.

  Nowhere to go.

      (**DELORES** *takes* **SAMANTHA**'s *hand in hers. She examines the lines.*)

  Let's see.

  This line that splits in two here? It means you can see the world from another's perspective. That's very true about you, I think.

  And this long curved line? That means you're passionate, you have deep desires.

      (**DELORES** *strokes* **SAMANTHA**'s *hand.*)

      (**SAMANTHA** *relaxes and takes a deep exhale.*)

  And this one. Ah. Only for the magnífico, the muy importante. This short line right here, strong and deep, mi angél, shows great vitality.

(DELORES *squeezes* SAMANTHA*'s hand and holds it still.*)

(SAMANTHA *drifts away to sleep.*)

Scene Six

(**SAMANTHA** *and* **LAYNE** *are in their respective homes.*)

(**LAYNE** *is wearing a long cotton nightshirt with cats on it.*)

(*It's late.*)

(*They chat online.*)

KINGDOMCOME42: mi angél

DELAYEDFLIGHT82: hi :)

DELAYEDFLIGHT82: what are you doing?

KINGDOMCOME42: i was waiting for you...

DELAYEDFLIGHT82: oh yeah?

KINGDOMCOME42: I'm always waiting 4 u.

KINGDOMCOME42: every single day, ur the first thought I think.

DELAYEDFLIGHT82: sorry i couldn't come on earlier, work was crazy today.

KINGDOMCOME42: its okay i was just worried I did something wrong

DELAYEDFLIGHT82: never. u r perfect to me.

KINGDOMCOME42: did you have a good day?

DELAYEDFLIGHT82: I couldn't stop thinking about that thing with your liver.

DELAYEDFLIGHT82: it really upset me.

KINGDOMCOME42: that's just ur anxiety babe. nothin 2 be worried about, ok?

DELAYEDFIGHT82: good

KINGDOMCOME42: u know I started doing those affirmations u gave me.

DELAYEDFIGHT82: really? im so glad you tried them. aren't they amazing?

KINGDOMCOME42: i've been feeling calmer.

DELAYEDFIGHT82: see?

KINGDOMCOME42: i still think it's bullshit

DELAYEDFIGHT82: that's cause you're a guy ;p

KINGDOMCOME42: but I wanted 2 bc u like it ;) i love when u teach me things.

DELAYEDFLIGHT82: wanna learn my mantra? I say it everyday.

DELAYEDFLIGHT82: i've nevr told anyone about it b4. do u think it's dumb?

KINGDOMCOME82: nothing you do is dumb.

DELAYEDFLIGHT82: okay, it goes: om namo bhagavate vasudevaya

KINGDOMCOME42: what does it mean?

DELAYEDFLIGHT82: "May I become all that I'm meant to be."

KINGDOMCOME42: om namo bhagavate vasudevaya.

KINGDOMCOME42: that's rly nice, court.

KINGDOMCOME42: maybe it can be our thing.

DELAYEDFLIGHT82: okay

KINGDOMCOME42: i'll do it everyday, too. then when we meet, we'll do it together.

DELAYEDFLIGHT82: I love that.

[SAMANTHA *smiles.*]

KINGDOMCOME42: so, did u just get home? how was italy?

DELAYEDFLIGHT82: it was amazing!!

DELAYEDFLIGHT82: I went to this famous museum and saw sculptures

DELAYEDFLIGHT82: and smoked cigarettes with an ex pat

KINGDOMCOME42: ur so cultured

DELAYEDFLIGHT82: i ate a fresh baguette this morning.

DELAYEDFLIGHT82: it melted in my mouth...

KINGDOMCOME42: maybe one day I can make 1 for u. i know i'll melt in your mouth.

KINGDOMCOME42: *it'll :)

DELAYEDFLIGHT82: how big is it?

DELAYEDFLIGHT82: ...your baguette :)

KINGDOMCOME42: ;)...

KINGDOMCOME42: i wish we were together right now, courtney.

KINGDOMCOME42: i wish I was holding u.

DELAYEDFLIGHT82: me too. i'm even wearing something special...

KINGDOMCOME42: really? don't tease me...

DELAYEDFLIGHT82: i am. i bought it today.

KINGDOMCOME42: u must look so sexy.

DELAYEDFLIGHT82: u r so sweet.

KINGDOMCOME42: u know how u make me crzy.

KINGDOMCOME42: I cant wait 2 feel ur body on top of mine, courtney.

DELAYEDFLIGHT82: me 2, dom...

KINGDOMCOME42: i'm getting hard just thinking about you in that little slip

> [Beat.]

> [LAYNE *feels nervous.*]

KINGDOMCOME42: is it ok that I said that?

> [Beat.]

DELAYEDFLIGHT82: ...how do u know it's a slip?

KINGDOMCOME42: i can see it. it's black with lace trim

KINGDOMCOME42: and it's sheer in the tummy.

KINGDOMCOME42: so I can kiss you through your clothes.

KINGDOMCOME42: that little tiny body.

KINGDOMCOME42: I hold u so tight.

KINGDOMCOME42: i tower over u.

DELAYEDFLIGHT82: I feel so safe in ur arms.

DELAYEDFLIGHT82: what else do u see?

KINGDOMCOME42: that freckle right next to your belly button.

KINGDOMCOME42: the one I love.

DELAYEDFLIGHT82: what else do u love...?

KINGDOMCOME42: i love how your breasts perk up when I kiss your neck.

KINGDOMCOME42: i like to feel them, all for me.

KINGDOMCOME42: I look into your beautiful eyes

KINGDOMCOME42: i see you, clearly. i see you, fully.

KINGDOMCOME42: i can taste you.

DELAYEDFLIGHT82: what else?

DELAYEDFFLIGHT82: tell me more.

DELAYEDFLIGHT82: i need to hear u say it...

DELAYEDFLIGHT82: i want to feel you with me, on top of me, your skin on my skin

KINDDOMCOME44: your skin on my skin.

DELAYEDFLIGHT82: yes...

KINGDOMCOME42: i pull your slip over your head

KINGDOMCOME42: i see your perfect body.

KINGDOMCOME42: you have goosebumps b/c it's cold.

DELAYEDFLIGHT82: you warm me up

DELAYEDFLIGHT82: you always make me feel so warm

KINGDOMCOME42: I feel your whole body...

KINGDOMCOME42: my rough hands, taking you, my strong body, moving with yours

DELAYEDFLIGHT82: yes...yes...

KINGDOMCOME42: I kiss your neck...your belly...your thighs

DELAYEDFLIGHT82: i fucking love when u do that.

DELAYEDFLIGHT82: i need u...

KINGDOMCOME42: I trace the lines of your body up and down, I press closer

DELAYEDFLIGHT82: closer yes closer

KINGDOMCOME42: so u can feel me.

KINGDOMCOME42: do u feel me wanting u

KINGDOMCOME42: wanting to be inside u

DELAYEDFLIGHT82: yes yes yes yes please come here please

KINGDOMCOME42: i slowly lick your neck and bite your ear.

KINGDOMCOME42: i feel u

DELAYEDFLIGHT82: yes

KINGDOMCOME42: i'm so close

DELAYEDFLIGHT82: uh huh

KINGDOMCOME42: ahh

KINGDOMCOME42: oh god

DELAYEDFLIGHT82: do that again

KINGDOMCOME42: fuck

DELAYEDFLIGHT82: don't stop

KINGDOMCOME42: you're so beautiful, Courtney.

KINGDOMCOME42: you're the most beautiful woman i've ever seen

KINGDOMCOME42: u should be told everyday. your amazing. your so special.

KINGDOMCOME42: u are everything to me.

DELAYEDFLIGHT82: I love you Dom I love you so much.

DELAYEDFLIGHT82: My whole life has been leading me 2 u.

DELAYEDFLIGHT82: I want to be with u 4ever.

[SAMANTHA *shuts the computer abruptly.*]

[*kingDOMcome42 has signed off.*]

[*The fantasy is over.*]

DELAYEDFLIGHT82: dom?

DELAYEDFLIGHT82: r u there?

Scene Seven

(Early morning.)

*(**SAMANTHA** is sleeping.)*

(She has drool dripping from her mouth.)

*(**DELORES** and **DOM** enter.)*

DELORES. Sammy! You awake?

*(To **DOM**.)*

Oh shh shh she's sleeping

DOM. I didn't say anything Mom you were the one screaming.

DELORES. Okay okay. Fix your shirt!

(She starts tucking his shirt into his pants.)

DOM. Ma! Get outta there!

DELORES. Sorry, sorry, I want you to look nice!

(She gives him a big kiss.)

(He recoils.)

DOM. Stop! Please!

DELORES. I just love you so much!

DOM. *(Sweetly.)* I know.

(They start to clean up as they talk.)

DELORES. See? Isn't this better than serving ritzy white people *ruggaloo?*

DOM. Ruggulah, Ma.

DELORES. *I* don't care!

DOM. You brought me to America! This is what you taught me!

DELORES. To be a busboy at a bakery?

DOM. *(Mimicking her accent.)* To follow my dreams!

DELORES. All I'm saying is there are places you can work here.

DOM. I HAVE TO LIVE IN LA!
THAT'S WHERE MY JOB IS!

DELORES. There are lots of jobs in Carson City!

DOM. What famous actors do you know who live in Nevada? Huh?

DELORES. Nicolas Cage.

DOM. I'M NOT TALKING TO YOU ABOUT THIS ANYMORE.

DELORES. Keep your voice down!

DOM. Don't you understand that I have dreams, Ma? I have a big life ahead. With a fulfilling career and a beautiful wife and a motherfucking Porsche.

DELORES. Language.

DOM. Don't you want those things for me?

DELORES. Of course! But I don't see any of them yet, that's all!

DOM. This is why I never come home!

DELORES. I just miss my baby is that so wrong?

DOM. They're paying me double what you make this week, got it?

DELORES. We'll work it out.

DOM. GOD BLESS AMERICA!

> *(**SAMANTHA** wakes up.)*

Shit.

Sorry.

> *(She sees **DOM**.)*

> *(She's groggy.)*

SAMANTHA. Oh.

Oh I thought – uh that he was – aren't you coming tomorrow?

Um.

Sorry.

> *(**SAMANTHA** sees **DOM** for the first time.)*

Hey.

DOM. Hey.

DELORES. Dom…this is Sammy.

And Sammy, this is Dominick Fernando Manuel
Aquendo.

DOM. Wait, I know you, yeah?

SAMANTHA. Um,
Yeah.

DELORES. What? What are you talking about?

DOM. We went to high school together, Mama.
Samantha Carlin.

SAMANTHA. You're lookin' at her.

DELORES. Huh??

DOM. Ma, don't you remember? We were partners for that
Civil War reenactment thing. She came over to the
house one time.

DELORES. Oh my.

> *(Beat.)*

I didn't recognize you, Sammy.

SAMANTHA. I know.

DOM. This is crazy, dude.

> *(He stares a little too long.)*

Good to see you.

DELORES. *(To* **SAMANTHA.***)* Why didn't you say anything?

SAMANTHA. I forgot.

DELORES. You forgot?!

SAMANTHA. It's not a big deal.
It was a long time ago.
Delores can I have my toothbrush?

DELORES. *(To herself.)* Eso está loco.

> **(DELORES** *exits.)*

> **(DOM** *stares at* **SAMANTHA.***)*

> **(SAMANTHA** *fixes her hair.)*

> *(A clump comes out.)*

SAMANTHA. Oh I uh
This wasn't supposed to

DOM. Here lemme get that.

SAMANTHA. No!

Oh no you don't have to –

I can –

(She tries to move around.)

(It's a struggle.)

DOM. Give it to me it's fine.

SAMANTHA. *(She smiles.)* Okay.

DOM. Man. It's been what, like fifteen years?

SAMANTHA. About that I guess.

It's cool what you're doing in LA.

DOM. Oh God what'd she tell you?

SAMANTHA. That you do commercials and magazines and stuff. Sounds awesome.

DOM. Well it's not. It's not awesome.

My mom doesn't fucking understand how hard it is. For me, it's about *the work*. *The craft.* Like would I take a job, *literally any job,* offered to me? Sure. But my passion is my process, you know? My acting class is like my family and my guru Chandra has changed my life. Anyway, most people in LA are just trying to make it big. They don't care about art.

SAMANTHA. Not everyone can be like you.

DOM. And what am I?

SAMANTHA. Special.

DOM. You're sweet. You get it.

SAMANTHA. You were always amazing in the plays and stuff. And on the morning announcements. That was my favorite.

DOM. "Hello Carson City High!

Dominick Aquendo here, and I'm giving you…your Morning Joe. Don't burn your mouth."

*(**SAMANTHA** and **DOM** both make the same gesture with their mouths.)*

Wow, Sammy!

That's cool.

I didn't think anyone ever caught that.

SAMANTHA. I did.

DOM. You have pretty eyes.

I never noticed them before.

SAMANTHA. Really?

DOM. Yeah. They're brown.

SAMANTHA. I know.

DOM. Like mine.

They're nice.

SAMANTHA. Thank you.

You do too.

Have a nice –

everything.

DOM. It doesn't feel that way back in LA.

Everyone is so good-looking.

SAMANTHA. Not here.

DOM. Definitely not here.

SAMANTHA. Maybe you should move home.

You'd be a supermodel.

Haha.

DOM. Haha.

SAMANTHA. Haha.

DOM. Haha.

SAMANTHA. Haha.

DOM. Anyway. I'm not moving here.

SAMANTHA. I know.

DOM. *(Re: the hair.)* I should toss this.

SAMANTHA. Right.

Thank you.

> (**DOM** *tosses the hair.*)
>
> (**DELORES** *walks back in with* **SAMANTHA**'s *toothbrush.*)

DELORES. So every time, Sammy, every time I talked about Dom, you just didn't say nothing?

DOM. Ma, drop it. She forgot. That's all. Right?

SAMANTHA. *(Twinkly.)* Right.

> (**DELORES** *hands the toothbrush over.*)
>
> (**DOM** *and* **DELORES** *watch* **SAMANTHA**.)

Um. Can I have a little…?

DOM. Oh!

Sure.

SAMANTHA. It's one of the few things I can do on my own, so –

DELORES. *(To* **DOM**.*)* She's nervous around you.

She always lets me watch.

> (**DOM** *and* **DELORES** *turn around.*)
>
> (**SAMANTHA** *brushes her teeth.*)
>
> (*She spits into a cup.*)
>
> (*She rinses her mouth with a cup of water.*)

SAMANTHA. All done.

DOM. Sweet.

DELORES. Let me get breakfast started.

You two get reacquainted, okay?

> (*To* **DOM**.*)*

be nice *y no seas cabroncito.*

> (**DELORES** *leaves.*)

SAMANTHA. Wanna watch TV?

DOM. Sure.

> (**DOM** *walks over to* **SAMANTHA** *and looks around for a place to sit.*)

SAMANTHA. You can just pull a chair over.

DOM. Cool.

> (**DOM** *pulls a chair over to* **SAMANTHA**.)
>
> (**SAMANTHA** *flips through the channels.*)

SAMANTHA. What do you like?

It's 9:15, so it'll be in the middle of a show.

Right now we have *The Chew, Live with Kelly,* and a rerun of *Jerry Springer.*

Family Feud comes on at 9:30 so we could find something to watch in the meantime?

DOM. You look really different than high school.

(*Beat.*)

Sorry.

SAMANTHA. It's okay.

DOM. You probably don't believe this, but I remember you at prom.

SAMANTHA. Really?

DOM. I remember you looked really pretty.

And I thought you were brave to wear that dress.

SAMANTHA. I don't think wearing a dress is considered bravery, but okay.

DOM. I just mean you didn't care what anybody thought.

And your dress was hot pink. It was cool.

SAMANTHA. I can't believe I never realized you were in love with me.

It all makes sense now!

DOM. Oh, yeah that's it.

SAMANTHA. Stalker.

DOM. I masturbate to you every night.

SAMANTHA. Should we like get married right now or something?

DOM. My mom can perform the ceremony. She's licensed in Colombia.

SAMANTHA. Our first dance might be hard, though, hon. I haven't seen my feet in years.

DOM. Don't you ever want to get better?

SAMANTHA. Wow.

DOM. You could die.

SAMANTHA. Mind your own fucking business dude.

DOM. All I'm saying is you can talk to me if you want. I'm a really good listener.

SAMANTHA. Thanks!

I'll let you know if I need a counselor.

DOM. I didn't mean to upset you.

SAMANTHA. You didn't. I've got brick walls up. Nothing gets to me.

So, what do you want to watch?

DOM. I like watching the TV Guide.

With the listings.

It's consistent.

I love that if I turn it on, and it's pretty far, ya know in the channels,

I can just wait a few minutes, and it starts at the beginning again.

> (**SAMANTHA** *looks at* **DOM**.)

Does that make me really lame?

SAMANTHA. Yeah.

> (*Beat.*)

Let's watch the guide.

DOM. Cool.

That way we can take our time deciding.

And by that time,

It'll be 9:30.

> (**SAMANTHA** *and* **DOM** *watch the channel-listings channel.*)

> (**SAMANTHA** *takes a picture of* **DOM** *with her phone.*)

What was that for?

SAMANTHA. So the cops know what happened to me when I get murdered.

DOM. At least lemme mug then.

> (**SAMANTHA** *takes a picture of* **DOM** *mugging for the camera.*)

Scene Eight

(Late night.)

*(*LAYNE *and* SAMANTHA *both lie in bed.)*

(They watch the channel-listings channel.)

DELAYEDFLIGHT82: this is nice

KINGDOMCOME42: it's my favorite thing to watch.

KINGDOMCOME42: it's important for things to be consistent. in this crazy world.

KINGDOMCOME42: u know?

DELAYEDFLIGHT82: when u know what to expect

KINGDOMCOME42: exactly. I love that u get me

DELAYEDFLIGHT82: I love that about us

KINGDOMCOME42: it's pretty special huh

DELAYEDFLIGHT82: were pretty special huh

KINGDOMCOME42: i'd say :p

DELAYEDFLIGHT82: I don't wanna go to work tomorrow

KINGDOMCOME42: play hookie! come visit

DELAYEDFLIGHT82: haha

KINGDOMCOME42: it's a short drive. just get in the car!

DELAYEDFLIGHT82: you know i don't drive, dom.

KINGDOMCOME42: just fantasizing. u know u can talk to me about it if u want.

KINGDOMCOME42: i'm a rly good listener.

DELAYEDFLIGHT82: thnx babe.

DELAYEDFLIGHT82: what should we watch now?

KINGDOMCOME42: my favorite movie is about to start!

DELAYEDFLIGHT82: omg i love when that happens.

DELAYEDFLIGHT82: what's your fav movie?

KINGDOMCOME42: its so random. im embarrassed

DELAYEDFLIGHT82: tell me

KINGDOMCOME42: promise u wont judge

DELAYEDFLIGHT82: of course

KINGDOMCOME42: ...

KINGDOMCOME42: the american president

DELAYEDFLIGHT82: shut up

KINGDOMCOME42: o god is that so lame

DELAYEDFLIGHT82: THAT'S MY FAVORITE MOVIE TOO

KINGDOMCOME42: NO

DELAYEDFLIGHT82: i used to watch it on vhs w/ my sister like everyday after school!!

KINGDOMCOME42: when she walks down the stairs

DELAYEDFLIGHT82: IN THE RED DRESS?!

KINGDOMCOME42: tears. streaming. down. my. face.

DELAYEDFLIGHT82: ARE U KIDDING ME.

DELAYEDFLIGHT82: where did u come from?

KINGDOMCOME42: ur dreams baby

DELAYEDFLIGHT82: I mean but ACTUALLY

KINGDOMCOME42: did u turn it on? its on amc

[We see the light of the TV reflected onto the women.]

DELAYEDFLIGHT82: I should send her some flowers

KINGDOMCOME42: You already did sir

DELAYEDFLIGHT82: i like watching tv w/u. it makes me feel like were 2gether...

KINGDOMCOME42: me 2.

KINGDOMCOME42: u make me the happiest person alive.

KINGDOMCOME42: do u know that?

DELAYEDFLIGHT82: I wish I could kiss u right now.

DELAYEDFLIGHT82: will u hold my hand?

KINGDOMCOME42: yeah

(**SAMANTHA** *puts her hand out to an invisible hand. She rests her head on an imaginary shoulder.*)

(**LAYNE** *puts her hand inside an invisible hand. She puts her head atop an imaginary head.*)

(*They sit for a while, watching the movie together.*)

Scene Nine

(*SAMANTHA is doing a photo shoot with* **DOM**.)

SAMANTHA. Yeah just tilt your head.

DOM. Like this?

SAMANTHA. That looks good.

DOM. What about like this?

(*He makes a "sexy" face.*)

SAMANTHA. You look constipated

DOM. (*Laughing.*) Hey!

SAMANTHA. Don't you want me to be honest?

DOM. Yes.

(**DOM** *continues to pose for photos.*)

SAMANTHA. Just be natural.

I'm getting some good shots here.

Yes.

Yes!

Work the camera.

Make love to the camera.

LET ME SEE THAT FACE!

Gimme those eyes.

That's it.

Smize.

That's right. I wanna know what else is hiding behind those baby browns.

More.

More.

A little too much.

No. Creepy.

Better.

Yes yes.

You're gonna love these, Dom.

DOM. Cool.

You're better than the professionals I work with.

SAMANTHA. Want me to upload them to my computer? I can just email them to you.

That way you'll have them when you're back in LA tomorrow.

DOM. You'd do that for me?

SAMANTHA. Sure.

It's easy.

(**SAMANTHA** *scrolls through the pictures.*)

DOM. How do I look?

SAMANTHA. Perfect.

DOM. You're awesome, Sam.

SAMANTHA. I know.

(*Beat.*)

DOM. So how long have you – uh –

SAMANTHA. What?

DOM. Been like –

SAMANTHA. Couple years after high school.

DOM. Cool.

SAMANTHA. It doesn't just happen overnight, you know.

My old therapist said I eat because food can't hurt me.

Then I get depressed so I eat more.

I think it's because I hate my mother!

DOM. So I guess this is like the ultimate rebellion, huh?

SAMANTHA. (*Amused.*) Yeah.

I've thought about getting that surgery? But it's really fucking expensive.

DOM. Then do something about it.

SAMANTHA. Oh yeah sure let me just lose three hundred pounds.

DOM. Start small.

(*Beat.*)

You know, you have a really pretty face.

SAMANTHA. Yeah right.

DOM. You don't think so?

SAMANTHA. No.

DOM. Have you ever had a boyfriend, Sammy?

(**SAMANTHA** *shifts.*)

You will one day.

SAMANTHA. How about you? Do you have a hundred girlfriends in LA?

DOM. I can't deal with most chicks I meet.

They're crazy.

But I do want a wife someday, for sure.

Someone who needs me to take care of her.

Just haven't met the right person yet.

SAMANTHA. We all need to be taken care of. To know that someone in the world *actually* gives a shit how our day went. And wants us to have a better day tomorrow.

It's kinda like my personal philosophy.

DOM. (*Exhale.*) Man, that's deep.

(*Beat.*)

SAMANTHA. This must be the worst job you've ever had. Babysitting some fat girl.

DOM. Loca, gain some confidence.

You can be whoever you wanna be.

Sit up tall.

(*She rolls her eyes but does.*)

Soften this here.

(*He gently rubs the space between her eyebrows.*)

(*She softens them.*)

Gimme a smile.

(*She does. A fake, cheesy one.*)

(**DOM** *is delighted by* **SAMANTHA**.)

SAMANTHA. You're being paid to be nice to me.

I have to keep reminding myself that.

DOM. Close your eyes.

> *(She does.)*

And see yourself how you imagine.

The way you want to be.

What does it look like?

SAMANTHA. I don't want to do this.

DOM. Come on.

Chandra taught me. It totally works.

> **(SAMANTHA** *peeks.)*

Keep your eyes closed.

Breathe.

Imagine your heart's a burning red that turns to orange.

SAMANTHA. What is this?

DOM. Shh. Go with it.

Let it transform into a beautiful blue. Imagine that blue moving to your throat –

SAMANTHA. Dom –

DOM. Morphing to a deep indigo.

Watch this move up to your forehead, and let it shoot up towards the night sky.

Do you feel better?

SAMANTHA. No.

DOM. Keep your eyes closed! Visualize!

SAMANTHA. Sorry!

DOM. I'll do it too.

> *(Beat.)*

Right now, I see an ocean. And I'm surfing on the waves you know, but I'm so still, like crazy grounded. And all the people I've ever known are all surfing too. But no one is falling off you see, we're just floating by each other. And we nod. Like, cool man. I *see* you. And in this moment *(He takes a deep breath.)* I feel totally connected to the Universe.

SAMANTHA. How do I do it?

DOM. Imagine your heart's deepest longing is already so. What do you see?

SAMANTHA. I see…

…

Me, running.

By a highway.

The wind blows my hair behind me and my ears catch the sounds of cars passing by.

I'm moving so fast. Superhuman fast.

My body is working. It's strong, useful.

DOM. Where are you going?

SAMANTHA. To pick up my daughter from school.

My beautiful, smart little girl. Her name is Hannah.

She wears a yellow dress. She won't ever let me take it off her!

I lift her up over my head.

She laughs a great big belly laugh.

I pull her into me, and we squeeze each other.

We never want to let go.

She looks just like me.

But also just like my husband, Calvin.

We're a perfect happy family.

Just like the kinds in the Macy's commercials.

Just like the kinds in the picture frames at CVS.

> (**SAMANTHA** *has tears running down her face.*)
>
> (*She keeps her eyes closed.*)

DOM. Samantha?

Hey, I'm sorry.

SAMANTHA. Calvin?

DOM. Huh?

SAMANTHA. Calvin, Hannah and I are off to ballet. Would you mind putting the pot roast in the oven?

DOM. (*Playing along.*) Uh, yeah, the pot roast.

SAMANTHA. I got it fresh from the market today. Don't worry about the sweet potatoes or the asparagus. I'll fix those up when I get home.

DOM. Well, I am very busy at the office today, I had two big trials, but we won the case, so everyone at the office threw me a party. For being such a good lawyer.

SAMANTHA. I bet you're gonna get a promotion.

Lacker, Bridgeport, and...

Hobbes: Attorneys at Law.

DOM. Who is Hobbes?

SAMANTHA. That's our last name.

DOM. Right. Calvin Hobbes.

SAMANTHA. And I have a surprise for you, darling. I've been planning it all week.

DOM. You do?

SAMANTHA. I picked up your favorite bottle of red. We can have a glass by the fire tonight after Banana goes to bed.

DOM. That sounds nice.

SAMANTHA. How did I get so lucky? How did I find a man like you?

DOM. How did I get so lucky? How did I find a woman like you?

SAMANTHA. That's my line.

DOM. Sorry.

> *(Beat. The fantasy is over.)*

That was fun.

You're a good actress.

You'd do super well at The Actor's Gym.

SAMANTHA. Great.

> *(SAMANTHA turns over on her side.)*

I'm tired. Can I be alone now?

DOM. Sam. I have something to tell you.

> *(DOM goes over to SAMANTHA to whisper something in her ear.)*

(This is the trick little boys play.)
(She turns around. He kisses her on the mouth.)
(**SAMANTHA** *lingers in this moment.)*

See you soon, Sammy.

Scene Ten

(**LAYNE** *and* **SAMANTHA** *chat.*)

(**LAYNE** *looks at the photos* **SAMANTHA** *just took of* **DOM**.)

DELAYEDFLIGHT82: u look so gorgeous in these!

KINGDOMCOME42: let me send a few more. they're uploading now.

DELAYEDFLIGHT82: whoever photographed u definitely made u feel comfortable

KINGDOMCOME42: thnx babe. i thought u'd like them. I took them all 4 u.

DELAYEDFLIGHT82: I'm gonna frame one next 2 my bed.

KINGDOMCOME42: when am i gonna get some of u?

KINGDOMCOME42: i've been so patient

DELAYEDFLIGHT82: u have some!

KINGDOMCOME42: some new ones...

KINGDOMCOME42: come on...i've memorized the ones you sent me

KINGDOMCOME42: ...i need something new...

DELAYEDFLIGHT82: okay. i'll take 1 n send it

> [**LAYNE** *frantically goes onto Facebook and screenshots the first picture of a blonde girl in a bikini she can find.*]

> [**LAYNE** *presses send.*]

DELAYEDFLIGHT82: voila!

KINGDOMCOME42: woah

DELAYEDFLIGHT82: thnx :)

> [**SAMANTHA** *examines the picture.*]

KINGDOMCOME42: uh

KINGDOMCOME42: u look kinda different here

DELAYEDFLIGHT82: o, probably the lighting

KINGDOMCOME42: cool. ur on the beach right now?

DELAYEDFLIGHT82: yeah

KINGDOMCOME42: b/c last night u said u were gonna be home for a few days

KINGDOMCOME42: so which is it

DELAYEDFLIGHT82: im in bali

DELAYEDFLIGHT82: i got called in on a flight

KINGDOMCOME42: o

KINGDOMCOME42: y didn't u tell me

DELAYEDFLIGHT82: it was super last minute. i forgot.

KINGDOMCOME42: i don't believe u

DELAYEDFLIGHT82: y? i'm tellin u the truth

KINGDOMCOME42: whatever.

> [SAMANTHA *gets angry.*]
>
> [*She feels like a big, huge, fucking idiot.*]

DELAYEDFLIGHT82: dom?

DELAYEDFLIGHT82: u thr?

KINGDOMCOME42: i have 2 go

DELAYEDFLIGHT82: please don't

KINGDOMCOME42: i just have 2 go ok

DELAYEDFLIGHT82: why r u being weird

KINGDOMCOME42: ?????

DELAYEDFLIGHT82: ur being cold

KINGDOMCOME42: i really don't feel like talking 2 u right now

DELAYEDFLIGHT82: y what did i do

KINGDOMCOME42: u lied

DELAYEDFLIGHT82: no I didn't

DELAYEDFLIGHT82: it happened last night my phone was dead and i couldn't get on til now

KINGDOMCOME42: y r u sending me pix that aren't u

DELAYEDFLIGHT82: that is me i just took it! whut r u talking about

KINGDOMCOME42: no u didn't it has a time stamp from 4 yrs ago

DELAYEDFLIGHT82: whut r u a fucking hacker now or something

KINGDOMCOME42: tell me the truth

DELAYEDFLIGHT82: it's me!

KINGDOMCOME42: y r u lying?!

> [LAYNE *is dumbfounded.*]

> [*She doesn't know what to say.*]

KINGDOMCOME42: HELLO

KINGDOMCOME42: HELLO HELLO HELLO HELLO

KINGDOMCOME42: COURTNEY I KNOW UR THERE

DELAYEDFLIGHT82: i'm sorry.

DELAYEDFLIGHT82: i'm so sorry.

DELAYEDFLIGHT82: dom

DELAYEDFLIGHT82: I don't know why i did this.

DELAYEDFLIGHT82: i wanted you to think I was pretty.

KINGDOMCOME42: r u serious

DELAYEDFLIGHT82: im so sorry i am so so sorry dom

KINGDOMCOME42: so none of these pics r u?

KINGDOMCOME42: who r u?

DELAYEDFLIGHT82: i'm the same person

DELAYEDFLIGHT82: it's still me

DELAYEDFLIGHT82: it's the same person

DELAYEDFLIGHT82: pls dom can we talk about this

DELAYEDFLIGHT82: hello???????

KINGDOMCOME42: is ur name even Courtney

DELAYEDFLIGHT82: yes

DELAYEDFLIGHT82: no

DELAYEDFLIGHT82: sorry

DELAYEDFLIGHT82: it's layne. layne falcone.

KINGDOMCOME42: um

DELAYEDFLIGHT82: i'm just gonna be super honest and like no more lies u know

KINGDOMCOME42: r u kidding me

DELAYEDFLIGHT82: im so sorry. i am so so so fucking sorry.

DELAYEDFLIGHT82: i didn't expect to fall in love on here I thought it was gonna be

DELAYEDFLIGHT82: i thought it was gonna be – a joke or just I dunno

DELAYEDFLIGHT82: a way to pass the time

DELAYEDFLIGHT82: but i love you I fell in love with u

DELAYEDFLIGHT82: and all the things I said I meant

DELAYEDFLIGHT82: and all the things I told u r true

DELAYEDFLIGHT82: I was afraid 2 tell u. once it started 2 feel real. i was afraid.

DELAYEDFLIGHT82: pls believe me. pls. i love u.

DELAYEDFLIGHT82: dom? pls answer me

DELAYEDFLIGHT82: please please please don't leave me please

DELAYEDFLIGHT82: i need u – don't go away – i need u

DELAYEDFLIGHT82: HELLO?????

DELAYEDFLIGHT82: DOM COME BACK

(**SAMANTHA** *closes her computer.*)

(*kingDOMcome42 has signed off.*)

Scene Eleven

(**LAYNE** *bangs on* **SUZ**'s *door.*)

(*It's three a.m.*)

(**SUZ** *answers wearing a little matching tank and pajama shorts, with an eye mask on top of her head.*)

LAYNE. Suz? Suz, come out here. Suz, are you there?

SUZ. Layne?

How do you know where I live?

LAYNE. Can you come out here? I have to talk to you about something.

SUZ. It's 3:00 in the morning.

> (*She steps outside.*)

Why are you at my house?

LAYNE. I need to borrow your car.

SUZ. What?

LAYNE. Please, can I just borrow it.

SUZ. (*This is not the sort of friendship they have.*) Um, I don't think so.

LAYNE. I don't have anyone else to go to. Please, I promise I'll take good care of it.

SUZ. Why don't you come inside.

LAYNE. No I have to leave right now that's what I'm trying to tell you.

SUZ. I'll make us some tea. Come on, Layne. It's cold. It's late.

LAYNE. I don't want any fucking tea.

SUZ. Woah. Okay.

LAYNE. Sorry.

SUZ. What's going on?

LAYNE. I have to go to to LA to see Dom.

SUZ. Right now?

LAYNE. (*Defensive.*) Uh, YEAH.

SUZ. You're going to get in a car in the middle of the night to meet a man four states away who you've never actually met.

LAYNE. Yes!

SUZ. That's crazy. Where are you going to stay?

LAYNE. I don't know, a motel?

SUZ. I thought you didn't drive.

LAYNE. I DON'T!

SUZ. Layne, you should really think about what you're doing before you drive a million miles away and get your heart ripped out of your chest. Don't you watch that show on TV? This never ends well.

LAYNE. I really don't think I should be taking advice from someone like you.

SUZ. Then why are you here?

LAYNE. Because I thought you were my friend.

SUZ. I'm trying to stop you from meeting some stranger who is going to chop you up into little pieces and murder you.

LAYNE. That's who you think I've fallen in love with?

SUZ. Fallen in love with?! What are you talking about?!

LAYNE. I have to take risks! This is my life!

SUZ. Layne, just come inside. Do you want to sleep over? We can get brunch in the morning.

LAYNE. NO!

SUZ. OH MY GOD I'M JUST BEING NICE. I really don't even care what you do. Just don't come back to Carson City whining about your anxiety and blah blah blah and how you need more medication.

LAYNE. That was one time!

SUZ. Because I *can't* call my dealer anymore, he tried to finger me last week, and also I think you're hiding from your real problems!

LAYNE. FINE! I WON'T! I don't know why I thought coming to you would be a good idea. I guess I figured you'd be understanding since you're fucking our married boss.

SUZ. Wow. I've told you a million times he's leaving his wife, Layne.

No wonder you have zero friends.

You're a very mean person.

LAYNE. Fuck you!

*(*LAYNE *starts to walk away.)*

SUZ. WHERE ARE YOU GOING?!

LAYNE. TO HERTZ!

SUZ. GOOD! I'm done. Do you hear me? I barely liked you in the first place. You're just the only other woman under sixty at work. And newsflash, I'd rather be friends with *Rhonda* from HR who has *literal sideburns* than *ever* talk to you again!

*(*LAYNE *leaves.)*

I hope you find what you're looking for, Layne.

*(*SUZ *screams after her.)*

AND I HOPE YOU PAY EXTRA FOR THE FUCKING GPS BECAUSE LA IS CONFUSING.

Scene Twelve

(**SAMANTHA** *signs online.*)

(*She takes a breath – she writes to* **LAYNE.**)

(*In this scene, chat dialogue should only be projected, not spoken.*)

KINGDOMCOME42: hi

KINGDOMCOME42: i don't even know what 2 say

KINGDOMCOME42: first i want to apologize for last night

KINGDOMCOME42: i was scared and i felt betrayed but i shouldn't have shut u out

KINGDOMCOME42: i'm sorry

KINGDOMCOME42: layne

KINGDOMCOME42: ...layne.

KINGDOMCOME42: its weird

KINGDOMCOME42: ur real name

KINGDOMCOME42: not that I don't like it

KINGDOMCOME42: it's a very nice name actually

KINGDOMCOME42: im just used to

KINGDOMCOME42: courtney

KINGDOMCOME42: and what that word has meant to me

KINGDOMCOME42: how I fill it up with you – all that you are, all that I love

KINGDOMCOME42: ur face, ur smile, ur nose

KINGDOMCOME42: the way ur lip curls up when ur happy

KINGDOMCOME42: and the way ur eyes open wide when ur caught off guard

KINGDOMCOME42: but really what I love most is

KINGDOMCOME42: ur heart

KINGDOMCOME42: ur sense of humor

KINGDOMCOME42: ur brain

KINGDOMCOME42: how u see the world

KINGDOMCOME42: how u lighten up my spirit

KINGDOMCOME42: and u make me feel like i'm enough

KINGDOMCOME42: like I can be my truest self w/ u and no matter what

KINGDOMCOME42: if I went bald

KINGDOMCOME42: or had one limb

KINGDOMCOME42: or lost all my teeth

KINGDOMCOME42: u would love me the same

KINGDOMCOME42: and that's what I want to tell u, layne

KINGDOMCOME42: I don't care where you've been

KINGDOMCOME42: or where u live

KINGDOMCOME42: or what ur job is

KINGDOMCOME42: or what you look like

KINGDOMCOME42: bc ur the most beautiful person I have ever met

KINGDOMCOME42: and I can't wait 2 love u forever and ever.

(**SAMANTHA** *closes her computer.*)

(*She shuts the light off next to her.*)

Scene Thirteen

(Night.)

(DOM is bussing the last few tables at Le Madeleine.)

(He wears a dirty white apron and a backwards cap.)

(He listens to headphones and sings along to the music in his ears.)

(LAYNE comes in the door of the bakery.)

(She sees DOM.)

(Her breath stops.)

LAYNE. Wow.

You're fucking real.

DOM. Oh shit.

(DOM removes his headphones.)

We're closed.

Sorry.

I forgot to lock the door.

We open back up tomorrow six a.m.

LAYNE. I can't believe I'm here.

That we're standing in the same room.

I am so unbelievably deeply fucking sorry for what I did to you.

It was the worst thing I've ever done. It's inexcusable. It's horrible.

And I just, I couldn't stop it. I thought about it. I tried. I thought about telling you the truth.

So many times.

But.

I got lost in our world, inside the little life we made together.

You trusted me and I lied to you, after –

after you've been so kind to me.

I've wondered what this would feel like – how I'd be, what we'd say to each other, how you'd look at me – which is sort of like I'm a crazy person – sorry, um I'm Layne?

DOM. Who?

LAYNE. Layne?

...

Courtney?

DOM. Sorry?

LAYNE. Courtney?

From online?

DOM. (*He looks at some paperwork.*) Uh, Courtney? I don't have anything written down. It's an online order you said?

LAYNE. I know I'm not as pretty as the girls in the pictures, but,

I'm the person you said you fell in love with.

And you know, I'll leave.

I'll just go.

And you'll never hear from me again.

But don't pretend that *this* didn't happen.

It was real to me, and I know it was real to you

If Courtney is who you want to remember.

Fine. I can handle it. I'm a big girl.

DOM. Lady I don't know what you're talking about.

LAYNE. Should I come back another time?

Or we could like go back to your place or something, where it's private.

DOM. Uh we're not going back to my place.

(**LAYNE** *moves toward* **DOM** *with an intensity.*)

Hey, back off, okay!

LAYNE. Why are you doing this to me, Dom?

DOM. You're really freaking me out.

And –

I'm gonna call the cops.

Yeah I'm gonna call the fucking cops if you don't get out of here.

Aaaand there's a gun,

on the premises and,

I've been cleared to use it if I need to.

So –

And I took a class once.

So –

Just go before we have any trouble okay.

LAYNE. *(Devastated.)* Wow.

DOM. Listen.

I don't know why you know my name.

Or why you're comin' in here talking about love or some shit.

Unless we slept together.

And I forgot.

Did we do that?

Sleep together and I forgot?

Because if so, I'm very sorry.

> *(Beat.)*

LAYNE. Are you online?

DOM. What do you mean am I online?

LAYNE. You know what I mean.

DOM. Everybody's online.

LAYNE. But do you online date?

DOM. Uh, no.

LAYNE. But like do you even have a profile?

> **(DOM** *shakes his head.)*

Oh God.

DOM. What?

LAYNE. Oh God.

DOM. What?

LAYNE. Oh my.

This is what –

Idiot.

IDIOT!

> *(To herself.)*

DID YOU REALLY THINK THIS WAS –

A *fucking good idea.*

Or fucking real.

You piece of dumb shit.

You are so disgusting.

STUPID! YOU ARE SO STUPID!

Oh God.

I –

I –

Am having –

A hard time –

> **(LAYNE** *takes sharp inhales.)*

DOM. Oh shit.

Come here.

Here, sit sit.

Let me get you some water.

Just like breathe.

Take deep breaths or whatever.

Uh –

> **(DOM** *shepherds* **LAYNE** *over to a table.)*

LAYNE. I think I have to throw up.

DOM. Don't do that.

LAYNE. I drove here.

From Nevada.

From Carson City.

I haven't driven in like –

and I well I have been very alone and very um *afraid* for
a long time now, and then I met you –

Well not *you*, but it was you, I mean it was Dom,

I think,

I thought –

I just –
I needed to see you,
or the person I thought you were,
are,
so I rented a car,
and,
I didn't stop.
I might even be on empty, I don't know.
I haven't driven in six years.
Or left the state.
Or um even done any fucking thing at all that's like mildly compromising.
And you aren't even you.
Well you're you, but you aren't him.
I have to go.
I have to leave.
I have to –

> *(She screams.)*

> *(Beat.)*

DOM. *(He registers what's going on.)* Oh shit.

LAYNE. And I just feel like,
    stupid,
    and,
    alone,
    and,
    hungry.
    My head hurts.
    The room is spinning.
    What am I doing here?

DOM. Do you want a grilled cheese?
    They're my specialty.

LAYNE. You really don't have to do anything nice.
    I should leave, actually.
    So I can like go kill myself or something.

DOM. Did you say Carson City?

LAYNE. Uh-huh.

DOM. My mom lives there.

LAYNE. *(Embarrassed.)* I know.

DOM. Jeez.

LAYNE. You probably think I'm a wack job.
But this is the first time I ever even tried online dating.
I just don't want to be alone forever.

DOM. Nobody does.

    (He remembers what **SAMANTHA** *told him.)*

I think we're all just hoping to find someone who cares
how our day went. And wants us to have a better day
tomorrow. It's sort of my personal philosophy.

    *(***LAYNE** *and* **DOM** *have a moment.)*

LAYNE. This might sound weird –
But
It still feels really good to see you.
Like, in person.
Is that weird?
That's weird.

DOM. What kind of sick fuck would do this?

LAYNE. Yeah I'd like to find out so I can –
Take action.
Take *legal* action.

    (She shudders.)

I am so skeeved out.
And you should be too you know.
Someone has done very *sexual* things to me.
As you.
Well, they've talked about –
Doing them.
And they've been done.
On your behalf.

DOM. How about for now we don't think about that part.
We'll deal with it later.

LAYNE. *(Smiling.)* Okay.

DOM. You got a nice smile.

LAYNE. No no no.

> (**DOM** *shakes his head "yes."*)
>
> (*He moves closer to* **LAYNE.***)*

You're very kind.

DOM. Do I look like how you imagined?

LAYNE. Exactly.

> (**DOM** *sits next to* **LAYNE.***)*

DOM. You're nervous.

LAYNE. I'm afraid you'll hate me.

DOM. How could I hate you? You're so adorable.

LAYNE. *(Flirty.)* I guess I have to like get to know you all over again.

DOM. Hey, you hear about the time I got lost at Disney?

LAYNE. We didn't get that far.

DOM. Oh, man, this is a good one.
It was at the *Honey I Shrunk the Kids* playground.

LAYNE. I love that place! We used to go every year!
The slides are so scary because you don't know where they end up.

DOM. Exactly! So I get dropped out on the wrong side, and my crazy ma is screaming in Spanish, tearing the whole place apart looking for me. We were on the national news. I was like *really* famous at school for the rest of the year. My mom tells this story like once a month.

LAYNE. Wow.
How did she find you?

DOM. She never stopped looking.

LAYNE. I don't blame her.

> (*Beat.*)

DOM. You come all the way from Carson City just to see me?

        (**LAYNE** *nods.*)

        (*Beat.*)

I bet you're hungry, querida.

LAYNE. Starving.

DOM. Grilled cheese offer still stands. You in?

        (**LAYNE** *nods. She smiles.*)

Scene Fourteen

(**SAMANTHA** *sits up in bed.*)

(*She searches online for Layne Falcone.*)

(*Hensher Insurance Agency, Inc. shows up.*)

(*She dials the number.*)

(*Lights up on* **SUZ,** *who is sitting at her desk.*)

(*The phone rings.*)

SUZ. Hensher Insurance, INC.

Suz speaking, how may I help you?

SAMANTHA. Um, hi.

I'm um looking for Layne Falcone?

Can I please speak with Layne?

(*Beat.*)

Does she work there?

SUZ. NOT ANYMORE, PROBABLY!

She's a dumb idiot and I hate her fucking guts.

I've been trying to cover for her all week because I'm a good person, but there's only so many lies I can tell.

I believe in Jesus!

SAMANTHA. Do you know where she went?

SUZ. Who is this?

SAMANTHA. Nevermind. Does she have like an extension? With a voicemail I could hear?

SUZ. No. Who do you think we are?!

SAMANTHA. Uh, I don't know.

SUZ. Do you want me to leave a note?

SAMANTHA. No, no.

That's cool.

Can you just tell me quickly – what is she um like?

SUZ. …What?

SAMANTHA. Oh, God. Nevermind. I have to go. Sorry.

(SAMANTHA *hangs up.*)

SUZ. Ugh. People are so goddamn rude.

Scene Fifteen

(SAMANTHA has an exercise DVD playing.)

(She's out of her bed and wearing a sweatband.)

(She tries to do some of the moves. She's not very successful, but she's up and at 'em.)

(SAMANTHA signs online to send LAYNE a message.)

(Next to DelayedFlight82 is a blank face, and the alert This Account Has Been Disabled.)

(SAMANTHA slams the computer shut.)

(Turns off the DVD.)

(Rips off her sweatband.)

(Gets back in bed. Rolls onto her side.)

(DELORES enters.)

DELORES. Samantha!

Samantha rise and shine baby girl, it's a new day and a new you, yes?

SAMANTHA WAKE UP!

I have something to tell you!

SAMANTHA. Shhh.

DELORES. Open those little babies!

(DELORES literally lifts SAM's eyelids off of her eyeballs.)

"LET THE SUNSHINE IN!"

SAMANTHA. Volume!

DELORES. Sorry.

I just can't stand the pouting anymore.

You're making me depressed.

SAMANTHA. Is it my job to entertain you?

DELORES. You are feisty this morning!

SAMANTHA. Can't I pay you to leave me alone?

DELORES. I'm already employed.

I gotta clean you up, Mamasita.

You smell like eggs.

SAMANTHA. I don't want to be bathed!

I don't want to be touched!

I want you to get the fuck out of here!

DELORES. What's going on?

Why can't you tell me?

SAMANTHA. You really wanna know, Delores?

DELORES. Yes!

SAMANTHA. *Dance Moms* is getting cancelled.

DELORES. Ay dios mio.

SAMANTHA. My dog is dying.

DELORES. What dog.

SAMANTHA. My hair is greying.

DELORES. Everyday, a new story.

SAMANTHA. I haven't eaten in three days!

Soon you'll walk in and I'll be doing yoga on the carpet.

DELORES. Sammy.

SAMANTHA. I'll be drinking green smoothies and measuring the gap between my thighs.

DELORES. Please.

SAMANTHA. There'll be a line around the block with only gorgeous men who want to fuck my brains out and love me forever.

DELORES. You're in rare form today.

SAMANTHA. *(In a Southern accent.)* Do I have any gentleman callers, Delores?

DELORES. Who?

SAMANTHA. Are there men lining around the corner for a piece of THIS?

> *(She grabs her hips.)*

Or this?

> *(She grabs her thighs.)*

Or this?

(She grabs her flabby arm.)

Or this?

(She grabs her tummy.)

DELORES. Samantha!

*(**DELORES** grabs **SAMANTHA**.)*

*(**SAMANTHA** screams in **DELORES**' face.)*

SAMANTHA. SAMANTHA SO FAT, WHEN SHE GOES TO AN AMUSEMENT PARK PEOPLE TRY TO RIDE HER! SAMANTHA SO FAT, SHE SAT ON A RAINBOW AND MADE SKITTLES! SAMANTHA SO FAT, THE ONLY ALPHABET SHE KNOWS IS KFC! SAMANTHA SO FAT, SHE WORE A YELLOW RAINCOAT AND PEOPLE YELLED TAXI!

(Beat.)

*(**DELORES** stares at **SAMANTHA**.)*

DELORES. I'll go make breakfast.

*(**DELORES** leaves **SAMANTHA**.)*

*(**SAMANTHA** pulls up DelayedFlight82's profile.)*

(It is still disabled.)

(She refreshes the page over and over and over again.)

(She slowly closes the computer.)

*(**DELORES** comes back out with a bowl of cereal.)*

(They are awkwardly silent for a beat.)

SAMANTHA. What did you have to tell me?

DELORES. We can talk about it later.

SAMANTHA. It's okay, Delores.

(Beat.)

DELORES. Dom is coming back to visit.

SAMANTHA. Why he was just here?

DELORES. Yes, but this time, he's bringing a *girl.*

And you'll never guess where she's from.

SAMANTHA. Where?

DELORES. Right here! In Carson City!

And how they met? It's the craziest story.

Some sick pervert pretended to be *my* Dominick on the websites and made a dating thingy what have you and met this nice girl on there.

SAMANTHA. Oh.

DELORES. She went to LA to find him!

SAMANTHA. She drove to LA??

DELORES. I don't know how she got there.

Anyway, Dommy was so *freaked out,* he was so *confused.*

I'm not surprised someone pretended to be him, he's gorgeous, but can you imagine a thing like this happened in real life?

SAMANTHA. No.

DELORES. It's a MIRACLE though because my Dommy is in love!

They haven't been apart since the moment they met.

I've never heard him talk about a girl like this before.

And they have gotten serious. *Very serious.*

SAMANTHA. How can you get serious in a few weeks?

DELORES. When you know you know!

SAMANTHA. So did they like find out who that person was or whatever?

DELORES. Not yet.

They put the search on hold for a little.

They're very wrapped up.

In each other.

SAMANTHA. Got it.

DELORES. Dommy and the girl are coming back to Carson tomorrow and they're going to stop by here! Dom wants you to meet her.

SAMANTHA. Why? Did he say why?

DELORES. You're friends, Sammy!

SAMANTHA. Delores, I really don't feel like having guests.

DELORES. Well, that's too bad, because I already cleared it with your mother.

SAMANTHA. What?!

DELORES. Sam, you haven't been yourself lately, and we need to pull you out of it.

A little company, a little party, won't hurt.

I even baked a special cake, my famous Torta Negra!

I even bought streamers and hats, all on sale from the Dollar Tree!

We can play Pin the Tail on the Donkey, that's Dom's favorite game.

OH! AND SAMMY GUESS WHAT?!

THERE'S GONNA BE A PINATA!!

Scene Sixteen

(**LAYNE, DOM, DELORES, SUZ,** *and* **SAMANTHA**
all wear party hats.)

(*There is candy on the ground.*)

(*A fast and furious Colombian song plays.*)

(**DOM** *leads* **LAYNE** *in a salsa dance.*)

(*They laugh and kiss and move swiftly around the
stage, in la-la love land.*)

(**DELORES** *tries to dance with them.*)

(**SUZ** *dances by herself in a very different style from
the rest.*)

(**SAMANTHA** *pouts and eats chips.*)

DELORES. Come on Sammy! Shake your hips!

SAMMY. I don't have hips.

DOM. Oh don't be a party pooper! Come on!
Que chimba de fiesta!

LAYNE. Que chimba de fiesta!

SUZ. YAAAAASSSS!

SAMANTHA. (*Regarding* **SUZ.**) Who the fuck is this?

DELORES. Layne's friend! Be nice!

SUZ. This is so totally bringing me back to Spring Break
senior year.
I spent most of it barfing on the floor of Señor Frogs,
but I had the most *fulfilling* time.

(**SUZ** *hugs* **SAMANTHA.**)

SAMANTHA. What are you doing?

SUZ. You looked like you needed a hug.

SAMANTHA. Touch me again and I'll strangle you.

SUZ. Oh my God, she is SO funny.
I'm hanging out with *her* all night!

(**SAMANTHA** *groans.*)

(**DOM** *dances over to* **SAMANTHA.**)

(He shimmies.)

DOM. Dance with me, mami.

SAMANTHA. I'm good.

>*(DOM takes SAMANTHA's hand and spins himself around. LAYNE slaps DOM's tush.)*

>*(LAYNE and DOM dance together again.)*

SUZ. LAYNE!

Look at you. You're so hot. You're like a totally different person.

LAYNE. Gracias!

SUZ. DENADA!

>*(To the group.)*

I took Spanish for twelve years in school.

DELORES. Suzie, I'm so glad you could join us!

SUZ. I *really* didn't want to go to work today.

DOM. Layne, do that move I showed you.

>*(She does.)*

LAYNE. Before I met Dominick I had two left feet. I could barely walk without tripping over myself. Total klutz.

DELORES. She's good, Dommy! For a *gringa*.

DOM. You gotta have rhythm to be with a Latin man, ain't that right Mama?

DELORES. That's right! And FLAVOR. This woman has flavor.

SAMANTHA. Which kinds?

DOM. Habanero.

DELORES. Uh-huh

DOM. And...cinnamon

DELORES. Delicioso!

DOM. And ginger. Because it's spicy and sweet...at the same time.

DELORES. My baby is a poet! You can see it in her eyes, too, right Sammy. A taste for adventure, a fervor for life!

DOM. *(Correcting her.)* Layne's got anxiety.

LAYNE. Um, it's just mild!

DOM. I've been helping her. Right, babe?

> **(LAYNE** *nods.)*

We've been doing my visualizations and she taught me a mantra that we practice together all the time.

SUZ. *(To* **SAMANTHA.***)* Layne is *so* spiritual.

DELORES. Ooh ooh teach us! I want a mantra!

DOM. Layne, come on teach everybody!

> *(He turns the music off.)*

LAYNE. Um, okay. It goes "Om namo."

DOM. Repeat after her.

DELORES & SUZ. "Om namo"

DOM. Sammy, do it with us!

SAMANTHA. No thanks.

DOM. *Come on.*

SAMANTHA. Om namo.

LAYNE. Bhagavate.

ALL. Bhagavate.

LAYNE. Vasudevaya.

ALL. Vasudevaya.

LAYNE. Now all together:

ALL. Om namo bhagavate vasudevaya.
Om namo bhagavate vasudevaya.
Om namo bhagavate vasudevaya.

DELORES. Wow.

DOM. This woman.

> *(He kisses* **LAYNE**'s *hands.)*

This woman makes me feel…! There are no words.

DELORES. *(In awe.)* Dommy.

SUZ. I'm so jealous I wanna kill myself.

DOM. Do you know what it feels like? To be this happy?

DELORES. *(On the verge of tears.)* No!

DOM. LIKE THE WORLD IS MINE!

> *(He howls.)*

I'M IN LOVE!

SAMANTHA. So, do you like to travel Layne?

LAYNE. I haven't done much but we really want to.

DOM. Yeah, we're gonna go to Paris!

LAYNE. And India.

DOM. And Colombia! I gotta show my baby off to all the cousins.

SAMANTHA. You seem like the type to want to travel. Go to museums. Eat baguettes.

> *(**LAYNE** looks at **SAMANTHA**.)*

LAYNE. For sure.

DELORES. Sammy's intuitive.

SAMANTHA. It's a gift.

> *(There's a strange weight in the room.)*

DELORES. So! Who wants more Fanta?!

SUZ. I'll help!

> *(**DELORES** and **SUZ** exit to the kitchen.)*

SAMANTHA. *(To **LAYNE**.)* Your mouth is orange.

LAYNE. Oh! Sorry. That's embarrassing.

DOM. Lemme at it!

> *(**DOM** grabs **LAYNE** and kisses her.)*
>
> *(His tongue is everywhere.)*
>
> *(**SAMANTHA** stares at them.)*
>
> *(**LAYNE** sees and stops him.)*

What's wrong?

LAYNE. Nothing.

So, Samantha, tell me about yourself.

SAMANTHA. What do you wanna know?

LAYNE. Well, um. What's your favorite color?

SAMANTHA. Red.

LAYNE. Cool.

What's your favorite, um, hobby?

SAMANTHA. I don't get out much.

LAYNE. Right. Well then, what's your favorite movie?

SAMANTHA. Can we change the subject?

DOM. Sammy, she's just asking you a question.

SAMANTHA. I don't wanna answer.

DOM. It's not, like, that personal.

SAMANTHA. I said I don't wanna fucking talk about this.

DOM. Jeez! What's riding your ass?

LAYNE. *(To* **DOM.***)* I'm gonna go help your mom. Um, get the soda.

(**LAYNE** *exits.*)

DOM. What's your problem? She's just being nice and you're acting like a bitch.

SAMANTHA. I'm just messing around.

DOM. So, do you like her?

SAMANTHA. I've known her for like twenty minutes.

DOM. But do you get a good feeling?

SAMANTHA. I don't know, sure.

DOM. Isn't it crazy how we met?

SAMANTHA. Yeah. Your mom told me.

DOM. I mean, this loon job shows up at my work, and I'm like "Who are you?" and she's like "I love you" and I'm like "Did I black out and knock you up?"

SAMANTHA. Romantic.

DOM. And she's like "Thinking about spending my life with you makes me want to live it, makes me less afraid."

SAMANTHA. She said that?

DOM. "I imagine our life together. Complete, perfect. Since meeting you, I suddenly feel like I could have a life worth living." Nobody has ever treated me like that before. Normally these girls just want me for my looks not what's *inside.* So I grabbed her and kissed her right there. And she just melted into me, Sam. It was like I was all of her fantasies coming true. I felt important. I felt like a porn star.

SAMANTHA. And you don't care that you're not the person she's talking about?

DOM. What do you mean?

SAMANTHA. That person she was talking about, who she said all those things about, isn't you.

(Beat. Something in DOM *changes.)*

DOM. Yeah, you wanna know who that is, Samantha? It's a disgusting loser who needs to take something that doesn't belong to them. To trick innocent, kind people for their own gain. I don't wanna know the kind of person who would do that. Because if I ever met them *(Intense, knowing.)* I'd put them down like a fucking dog.

*(*DOM *stares into* SAMANTHA*'s eyes, predatorily, aggressively.)*

(They are there for an uncomfortable moment.)

(Then LAYNE *comes back in.)*

LAYNE. Sam, you never answered my question. What's your favorite movie.

SAMANTHA. *(Still staring at* DOM.*) The American President.*

(Beat.)

LAYNE. Oh.

DOM. We were just talking about that sick fuck who pretended to be me.

It's so creepy. Right, Sammy?

LAYNE. I don't think it is.

DOM. What are you talking about? Of course you do.

LAYNE. I just mean that I understand. Maybe you're afraid to be yourself. Maybe no one ever made you feel worthy, but you're this amazing person, who has so much to give, and this is your only option. I get why someone would do that. You can't choose who you fall in love with.

(There's a quiet in the room.)

DOM. You're delirious from all that salsa, babe.
MAMA! WHERE'S THE FANTA?!
Be right back.

*(**DOM** kisses **LAYNE** and exits to the kitchen.)*

*(**SAMANTHA** and **LAYNE** look at each other.)*

SAMANTHA.
"THEY'RE CONGREGATIN' FOR ME AND MY GAL,
THE PARSON'S WAITIN' FOR ME AND MY GAL,
AND SOMETIME WE'RE GONNA BUILD A LITTLE HOME
FOR TWO, OR THREE, OR FOUR, OR MORE,
IN LOVELAND FOR ME AND MY GAL."

*(The lights shift to focus on **LAYNE** and **SAMANTHA**.)*

("For Me and My Gal" plays.)

(They see each other.)

*(**SAMANTHA** leaves her bed.)*

(The two women slow dance together to the song.)

*(**SAMANTHA** is light on her feet.)*

*(**LAYNE** holds **SAMANTHA**.)*

(The music swells.)

Scene Seventeen

(Late night.)

(Very little light, perhaps only the screens of the computers.)

(LAYNE and DOM are in bed. DOM is sleeping naked next to LAYNE.)

(He's splayed all over her. He snores.)

(She tickles his back.)

(She stares at his beautiful body.)

(SAMANTHA signs online and check's DelayedFlight82's profile.)

(It's been reactivated.)

(DelayedFlight82 gets a notification:)

(KingDOMcome42 is checking out your profile.)

(LAYNE sends SAMANTHA an IM.)

DELAYEDFLIGHT82: hi
KINGDOMCOME42: hey
DELAYEDFLIGHT82: how are you?
KINGDOMCOME42: i'm okay

[Beat.]

DELAYEDFLIGHT82: what are you doing up?
KINGDOMCOME42: can't sleep.
DELAYEDFLIGHT82: me neither.
KINGDOMCOME42: r u alone?
DELAYEDFLIGHT82: do u want me to be?
KINGDOMCOME42: yes.
DELAYEDFLIGHT82: then i am.
KINGDOMCOME42: is he awake?
DELAYEDFLIGHT82: dead asleep. snoring like a geezer.
KINGDOMCOME42: ha
DELAYEDFLIGHT82: ...

DELAYEDFLIGHT82: i miss u.

DELAYEDFLIGHT82: sorry.

>   *[Beat.]*

DELAYEDFLIGHT82: u there?

KINGDOMCOME42: i'm here.

KINGDOMCOME42: what r u wearing?

DELAYEDFLIGHT82: My cat pjs

KINGDOMCOME42: wanna watch tv?

DELAYEDFLIGHT82: okay.

>   *[They both put the TV Guide channel on.]*

>   *[They sit in silence for a minute.]*

DELAYEDFLIGHT82: the price is right is on.

DELAYEDFLIGHT82: let's watch

>   *(They both change the channel.)*

>   *(We see the light of the TV reflected onto their faces.
>   We hear an old clip of* The Price is Right.*)*

BOB BARKER. *(Voice-over)* "Hole Putt! Now you just relax.
That's right, line it up, and put that thing in that hole
and I'll give you that car. Now just a moment – what'd
you say?"

GIRL. *(Voice-over)* "I've never been so nervous!"

BOB BARKER. *(Voice-over)* "Oh, just relax. Just relax. You can
do it. You can do it."

>   *(She putts. It goes in!)*

>   *(Ding ding ding ding ding!)*

"YOU DID IT! YOU DID IT! YOU WON A CAR! YOU
WON A CAR!"

GIRL. *(Voice-over)* "AHHHH!"

>   *(Cheering!)*

BOB BARKER. *(Voice-over)* "Now you're not nervous! Now
you're ecstatic! Yeah! Yeah!"

KINGDOMCOME42: wanna watch something else?

DELAYEDFLIGHT82: its late

KINGDOMCOME42: okay

DELAYEDFLIGHT82: i should go to sleep

KINGDOMCOME42: okay

DELAYEDFLIGHT82: ...

KINGDOMCOME42: ...

DELAYEDFLIGHT82: i was sad not to have you

KINGDOMCOME42: but you have the real thing now

DELAYEDFLIGHT82: i guess.

KINGDOMCOME42: you got what you wanted.

DELAYEDFLIGHT82: it's not that simple.

KINGDOMCOME42: why?

DELAYEDFLIGHT82: he's not you.

DELAYEDFLIGHT82: he's a gross boy.

> *[They both laugh, maybe through tears.]*

KINGDOMCOME42: it's ironic, huh.

DELAYEDFLIGHT82: what is?

KINGDOMCOME42: my whole life I wished I was someone else.

> *[Beat.]*

DELAYEDFLIGHT82: me too.

> *[Beat.]*

KINGDOMCOME42: Goodnight, Layne.

DELAYEDFLIGHT82: Goodnight, Sammy.

> *(Both women shut their computers.)*
> *(The lights go completely out.)*

End of Play

www.ingramcontent.com/pod-product-compliance
Lightning Source LLC
Chambersburg PA
CBHW070350120726
47909CB00008B/2787